Dead of Night

Tales of the supernatural and the macabre

W R Todd

Table of Contents

Whitaker House Curse   3

I'm Still Alive   46

Jack   102

The Thing in the Shadows   121

Bumps in the Night   218

It's Just Johnny   230

The Whitaker House Curse

1

December 23, 1902: the last entry in the diary of Jules Croft

I must confess that for someone who is about to die, writing in my diary is a most odd notion. However, since there is no form of self-defense, no diminutive space on earth in which I can hide that will keep me from this terrible fate, I must do what comes naturally — I must write.

Being a man of middle age and a widower of nearly six years, writing gives me a chance to converse with my beloved Joan. She never answers me, of course, but I know the spirit of my dearest reads what I write, nonetheless. It comforts me to know that, and I must do what comforts my soul. These few words will be my last comfort — in this life and the next.

It is almost midnight. The witching hour. The winds howl outside my home. Their coldness has breached the window I now sit by; they betray the one who is, no doubt, waiting anxiously in the eldritch comfort of the shadows outside, counting down the minutes to my doom. At the appropriate time he will enter and begin to search the rooms, one by one, until he has found the only one occupied. That room is my room, and the Devil himself will be here to collect on a debt.

There is great debate in theological circles as to what the Devil looks like. Can he take the shape of a mere human, or is he the cloven hooved monstrosity portrayed in so many paintings and pictures? I have seen both diabolical manifestations of that most fallen of angels. And even at this very moment, as I hear the deliberate, hollow clapping on the cobblestone in the street below my window, I know which form he takes this night.

The intruder is not far off. He is eager to take what is his, so I must hurry to put to paper the events that precipitated this dreadful event:

This strange story began one year ago this very night. I had only been living in my current home a month, having decided that a change in scenery of a new home in a new village would help keep my thoughts away from how lonely I'd become since my wife's passing.

As I strode down the oak-lined avenue at the edge of the village proper, which I did daily to take in the crisp air and hopefully become acquainted with my new neighbors, I occasioned a peek at the dreary Whitaker House. It was a long neglected and empty manor house from which I most times shaded my eyes, partly because of its fall into ill repair, but mostly because it was a large, forbidding structure that looked more akin to a mausoleum than a home. I noticed on this brief glance that the double doors into the great house were ajar.

I stood momentarily, pondering the notion that the manor had at last fallen into someone's hands. I must admit, though, that the house looked as uninviting as ever it had, as the snow that would later blanket the drive and clothe the trees now stood suspended in gray blankets over it.

There were busy noises coming from within, so I crossed the cobblestone lane, passed the rusty, iron gates, and walked up the immense stairs to greet a fellow newcomer to the village.

My ears had not betrayed me. I looked in on busy workmen throughout, painting, washing, sweeping, and taking measurements of this thing and that. I asked one of the workers nearest the doorway if he was privy to the owner's whereabouts. He only shook his head in the negative and continued his sweeping.

Just then, a surprise came from around the corner of the door. I assumed by the robe he was wearing that it was one of the monks of Sutherland Abbey, the only religious order for miles, which one could get to straightway by traversing the moor at the back of the Whitaker House property.

A bright smile emerged from under his flowing, red beard. "Ah, good afternoon, Mr. Croft. Did I frighten you?" he inquired with a thick Scottish lilt.

I was a bit taken aback by the abrupt appearance of the bear of a man but said, "Not at all, my dear friar. I must ask, though, how you knew who I am. I don't recall having met you previously."

The large Scotsman chuckled. "Chin wagging of newcomers to the village spread quicker than butter in July — that and the fact that I know every face in the village, except for yours and our new tenant. It led me to the assumption that you, good sir, were the Mr. Croft I've been hearing about."

"Couldn't I have been the new owner of Whitaker House?"

He lost his hand in his beard as he scratched out a thought. "You could have been, but then you wouldn't have asked that worker, there, of the owner's whereabouts."

My face became flushed and I smiled. "I didn't know you had heard that."

"There's something to be said for honesty, he said, passing along a wry grin of his own. "I could have kept that secret and let you relish my astounding psychic prowess."

I bowed in mock humility. "I surrender to your abilities, nonetheless."

We shook hands, and he introduced himself as Brother Geoffrey.

Afterwards, I looked beyond his broad shoulders and said, "I hope the new owner doesn't mind a stranger stopping by to offer a 'hello'."

The burly monk motioned for me to enter fully into the confines of the house. "Am I to assume, then, that you haven't received an invitation?"

"Invitation? No."

"Well, that is why I'm here — to thank the good master of the house for the invitation to dinner and wish him well-needed good tidings. Ah, but matters seem to have him elsewhere, at the moment, so I've been admiring the renovations."

Of course, I had never seen the manor but from the outside, so I asked if the friar could take me on a tour, as we waited for the new owner to show.

Brother Geoffrey took me past the workers to a portion of the house that had been restored already or needed no work for its splendor to shine through. The banquet hall delighted me particularly with its large mullioned windows with colorful, quarrel-pane lattices, and intricate moldings. Many portraits of regally-attired ladies and gentlemen, some still half concealed by white dust covers graced the spaces between the floor-to-ceiling windows. A large yet-to-be-adorned Christmas tree stood in the far corner, next to an immense hearth.

The dwelling looked much more inviting within than its exterior would indicate.

From there we went into a dark-paneled library, whose shelves were being cleaned and restocked with numerous volumes—law books and the such, mostly, from what my quick glances could make out. At the far end, next to a small fireplace, whose crackling fire brought some much needed warmth to the room, was a low, arched doorway.

It seemed from the beginning of our tour that Brother Geoffrey purposefully led me to where we now stood.

"Do you know the history of this house?" he inquired.

"Just what little I've been given since my arrival," I replied. "I know this place has a dark past—devil worship, black Masses, nefarious things of that sort. But the true facts surrounding it have been lost, I fear."

The friar smiled at me once more, but it was not a smile of favor. It was a smile of mischief. "Follow me below, and I will relay the story of this house's evil past."

With a bit of reluctance but equal curiosity, I followed close behind, as we made our way down a narrow, gray-stoned stairway into a sunken study. The room to which he led me was small yet inviting. It had an small but flamboyantly carved chimneypiece, mahogany paneling with extraordinary etchings, a dusty, stained, dark marble floor, and one tiny stain-glassed window, which gave the room its only light besides what little filtered down from the library above.

"Do you know what this room is?" he queried with an odd tone in his voice.

"Can't say that I have any idea whatsoever," I replied as I gave the room a more studious eye.

The friar pulled on his luxurious beard as he said, "Then whatever gossip that has made its way to you must have been a corruption, for any good story of the house would not have neglected the happenings in this room."

"Please tell me, then. I am all ears."

"As I recall," the friar started, "the house was built by Sir Montrose Whitaker, Earl of Aylesworth, in the 1400's. He gained his wealth and power by making a pact with Lucifer himself, for Sir Whitaker was not the most capable of men, physically or mentally. During an uprising in which he had taken part, he was thrust through by a Scottish claymore and was mortally wounded. As he lay dying, the Devil came to collect his recompense for the pact. Sir Whitaker pleaded for more time. The Devil healed him and gave him six days to get his affairs in order, at which time he would return.

"Now I must say at this point in the story that Sir Whitaker was married to a fine, Christian woman. She was beautiful, loyal to her husband, and possessed a cunning not often seen in the fairer sex. Sir Whitaker reluctantly imparted the sad details to his wife of the pact made many years prior, and the Prince of Darkness himself would be back soon to take his soul.

"After six days, the Devil returned to the very spot on which we stand to take what was his. Sir Whitaker and his wife pleaded unceasingly for mercy."

"The Devil said, '*I must have recompense for our barter*'."

"The wife replied, '*Anything but his soul*'."

"The Devil, being of the most evil cunning, then said, '*There is one thing I will take that is not his soul*'."

"She said, '*Whatever it is, it is yours*'."

"'Sign this parchment first so we are bound that what I want – that is not his soul – is rightfully mine'."

"Sir Whitaker and his wife both signed a large, worn parchment that was written in a language neither could decipher. Since it wasn't his soul the Devil now wanted, they assumed they could confront whatever Beelzebub sought without fear of Sir Whitaker spending eternity in hell."

My eyes were as large as a jack-o-lantern's, and my mouth stood agape. "What, what did that wily serpent want?"

The friar smiled underneath his red covering. "He wanted five pounds of flesh."

"There is no way a mortal could deliver such a ware without giving up the ghost."

"Precisely," said the friar. "But the woman, being sly herself asked, '*Does handing over what you now want nullify all previous deals?*'"

"'*Absolutely,*' the Devil said. '*Give me what I want now, and all other previous barters are voided. It says as much in the document you signed.*'"

"'*Very well,*' said the wife."

"But as the Devil was about to exact his payment, the wife then said, '*There is no mention in that document we signed about blood being part of the payment, correct?*' "

"'*That is true,*' the Devil replied perplexed.

"She then smiled and said, '*Then five pounds of flesh you may have. However if but one drop of blood is spilled, the contract we signed is no longer valid.*' "

I gasped at the woman's quick thinking.

Brother Geoffrey continued, "Well, having been outwitted by Sir Whitaker's wife, the wily serpent went on his way empty handed."

I was astonished at the story. "Certainly, *that* tale was never relayed to me."

"I would expect not. Those details have been lost over the years. But the story is not over."

"What else could there be?"

"Eventually, Sir Whitaker's evil covenant was found out. A housekeeper, given over to the sin of gossip, had overheard the entire encounter between the couple and the Archenemy. Because she had freed him from the pact, Lady

Whitaker was set free, but Sir Whitaker was burned at the stake in the village square. Consumption took Lady Whitaker only a few years later, and the house, though passed on several times, has not had a stable occupant since that time."

"What had made all the previous owners leave?"

"They say that Lucifer himself comes back to trick the owners into giving up their souls as recompense for being outwitted by Lady Whitaker."

"Do you believe such a fantastical story?" I inquired.

He laughed a great belly laugh. "Of course I do! I've seen the handiwork of the Devil personally, so I am inclined to believe in its authenticity. Not to mention that this is all written down in a volume at the monastery."

"I'm not one to pass judgement on the supernatural — I acquiesce to your judgement on these things — but to me it sounds a bit far-fetched."

The friar gave me a sullen look and replied, "It is possible that the particulars may have been...exaggerated, but know this: it is verifiable that six times from that time to this, within one year of this place's occupancy, someone within the walls of this house or closely related to its owner has been found dead. As a religious man it is my duty, then, to warn the new owner of this house's dreadful curse."

I do not know if the eerie story had sobered my conscience after a delay, or if it was the look of utter confidence of the story's authenticity that radiated from the friar's bright blue eyes that made me believe. But with little doubt, I finally concluded that the ill events had actually transpired.

It was then that I no longer felt comfortable in the old home's embrace.

Suddenly, there was an echoing *click* at the door at the top of the stairs.

I said, "I am willing to bet that is the master of the house finally arrived."

Just as I said those words, a raven-haired gentleman, perhaps a few years past the age of thirty, with a neatly trimmed mustache and beard, appeared at the top of the staircase. A cane with an ornately carved handle was clasped in his right hand, and he used it to help steady himself as he descended.

"Hello, good sir," said Brother Geoffrey cheerfully, seeming to brush aside the very morbid conversation that had just taken place.

The man smiled in return and bowed slightly. When he spoke, the words issued slowly from his mouth with a dialect I have never before heard. "Hello. I apologize for my absence. The house is quite large, and I don't get around as well as I once did. I found myself at the end of the south wing when word was sent that company had arrived."

His voice mesmerized me. It sounded not unlike the lower notes on a great calliaphone—melodious, yet it had a sense of immense power. And his deep eyes pierced me when he turned and greeted me with the same slight bow he just given to Brother Geoffrey.

I said, "I am Jules Croft and this is Brother Geoffrey from the monastery. I hope you don't think us too forward, but the good friar took me on a tour of your beautiful home, since I am new to the village and haven't had the opportunity to know the place but from the outside."

He waved off the statement with a sweep of his free hand. "I have no ill of that, as I must say I was doing much the same. It will be some time, I fear, before I've seen the whole place, myself."

The burly Scotsman interjected, "I have come at your request, good sir, and I must confess, a dinner is a fine way to christen new life back into this most ancient of homes."

"I am glad you've accepted my invitation." He then turned to me. "And you, Mr. Croft, are here for the dinner, as well?"

"I apologize, but I knew of no dinner or invitation to such. I was just out strolling the avenue and saw your worker bees turning this tired old place to honey."

"Please, stay and dine with us. I would feel much at ease knowing that there was at least one more person in my company that knows as little of this quaint corner of earth as I do."

I nodded and said, "I'd love to…I don't believe I caught your name."

His face became flush with embarrassment. And I must confess that, looking back, its redness seemed uncannily natural on him.

"Please forgive my ill manners. My name is Victor. Victor Strigoi."

"Where is your country of birth, if I may be so forward?"

"I am from Carpathia."

Brother Geoffrey, ever pulling at his whiskers, said, "I have done some missionary work in that part of the world — Galacia and the area around. Where, exactly, did you live? Maybe I have been there."

Mr. Strigoi only frowned and said, "It is a small village. I am quite sure you have never heard of it."

Though he didn't inquire any farther, I could tell at the time that there was something quite sobering that Brother Geoffrey was pondering silently. By the tension visible on the only skin not hidden by whiskers, I knew that at some point this topic would be revisited.

After an awkward moment of silence, Mr. Strigoi offered, "Others will be arriving soon. May I ask that we go above and await their arrival? I would hate for others to suffer the same impoliteness that I have shown you."

We waited for our host to ascend the steps before we marched up behind him. During that brief interval I whispered to the friar, "When will you tell him of the house's curse?"

"The time is not yet right," he rebutted softly. "He has put much into this dinner, and I will let it play out before warning him. I don't have to tell you that once I have given caution that is all I can do. The choice will be his to make whether he stays or goes."

I shuddered as we walked up the staircase back to the library above. "If what you say is indeed true, and this house is cursed, as it truly seems, I pray that he heeds your warning."

"I am praying the very same thing, even as we now speak."

2

Once at the top of the stairs, Mr. Strigoi motioned to the library entrance door. "Please, can I offer you a glass of wine while we wait for our other guests?"

Brother Geoffrey smiled behind his whiskered mask and his eyes lit. "Never let it be said that a monk willingly passed up a warming sip of wine, especially on a day as raw as this."

I nodding obligingly, as well, and our host went to an empty bookshelf next to the entrance where, oddly enough, a bottle of wine had been sitting along with two glasses.

"Two woodcarvers had done a remarkable restoration to the mantelpiece here in the library," he began to explain, as he poured one then the other glass with the deep, red liquid, "and I had offered the wine to them. However, when I returned with the wine and glasses, they had disappeared."

Though I didn't mean to, I can only assume that my gasp was audible, for both the friar and our host turned to me with upturned brows. It seemed my inward misgivings of the place has seeped to the surface.

Mr. Strigoi's laugh was like fingers dancing across the lower octaves of that great organ of which his voice reminded me. "You look as though I had just informed you that the woodcarvers had been killed."

I swallowed hard, not knowing what to say. Finally, I asked, "What happened to the poor souls?"

He handed each of us our glass and said, "I had been informed that the *poor souls*, as you so put it, had another job they were hoping to get done before Christmas and did not have time for socializing. It seems I had kept them here longer than anticipated."

Wanting to change the subject, I said as I took my first drink, "I see by the abundance of law books that your profession is law."

"Yes. I attended University at Edinburgh. Sadly, there are very few opportunities in my native land for such a vocation, so I decided to practice in the land that so graciously taught my profession."

Brother Geoffrey was devouring his glass of wine as we conversed. His thirst seemed insatiable. Had I not looked around at the grand display of volumes as we spoke and noticed him take his last swallow, I would have ventured that the monk never had his goblet filled. After he had taken his last swallow and gave a slight reverberation, he said, "That was the best wine, outside the Blessed Cup, I think I have ever put to my lips."

Mr. Strigoi expressed a sly grin and poured more into the friar's glass, as I, too, took a more scrupulous drink and came to the same conclusion. "I must say, I agree. This is absolutely delightful."

"Tell me," Brother Geoffrey insisted, "where can a man get their hands on such a lovely bottle of wine?"

"I am in possession of the only bottle left of its kind."

"Having only one bottle in the world of such perfect wine is blasphemy," he replied, as he savored more slowly his second glass. "This is heaven."

"How did you come by it?" I asked.

"I was told by the old man through whom I came to possess this bottle that in ancient times, Jews rarely finished a bottle of wine at the table." He then pondered us a thought: "What must have happened to the wine from The Last Supper if it hadn't been entirely consumed?

After a moment of contemplation, Brother Geoffrey replied, "Surely they drank it at a later date. Another meal, perhaps."

Mr. Strigoi rubbed his manicured whiskers thoughtfully. "Perhaps. But as a religious man of that most ancient of faiths, you should know that the early Church saved everything it considered holy. You have the bones of your saints under every altar of every church. They saved wood from the Cross; the vail which wiped your Savior's face, nails from the crucifixion—all saved. Could they not have saved the wine? *Wouldn't* they have saved it? Might that unlabeled bottle resting on the bookshelf be…?"

Everything went quiet at the utterance of that last statement, as if everyone were thoughtfully regarding such a terrific story. I remember in that brief silence a strong wind buffeting the library window. It was of such force that even the fire in the fireplace could not subdue the cold December that momentarily seeped into the room.

Suddenly, Mr. Strigoi let out an uproarious laugh, and the friar followed suit. Not wanting to be left out of a joke that I was not privy to, I laughed as well.

Brother Geoffrey, choking back laughter and wine offered to me, "It seems our host is quite the story teller, Mr. Croft. This should be a lovely dinner, indeed."

I nodded in agreement then turned to the owner. "Will you not get a glass and have a drink with us, as well?"

His face turned sour. "I don't drink it," he replied. "Although it is palatable to you, it doesn't agree with me. My taste is for — darker, stronger spirits."

We chatted a bit longer while we finished the wine then proceeded to the banquet hall, as one of the servants set the large hearth aflame; soon the entire room was filled with warmth and a golden glow.

Within the hour, the workers were excused for the day and shortly thereafter, guests started to arrive. There was Mr. Oglevie, the butcher, and his wife and children, Ms. Danner, a fine, young woman who ran a floral shop in the village square, the town doctor, Nigel McGinty and his wife and children, along with several others whom I had never personally met before.

The total for dinner, myself included, was seventeen.

Now, just as the last guests arrived — two associates from the law firm in the city where Mr. Strigoi practiced —

the heavens let loose with the snow they had, since early morning, been so reluctant to release. With the white drapery came howling winds that rushed around the manor house, making a clamor like the shrieking of a legion of ghosts. Though it was only four in the afternoon, with the hidden sun already nearing the horizon, the sky grew the color of slate.

Looking back on those events, it was certainly a harbinger of things to come.

Since no one knew better at the time, we all gathered in the banquet hall for hors d'oeuvres that the servants had set out. It was fine fare that whetted our appetites for the evening meal to follow.

We all laughed and enjoyed the company of old — and new — friends, and the children laughed and giggled as they set about decorating the giant evergreen tree for the holiday.

While chatting with the good doctor McGinty about a persistent lower back ache, I per chance noticed Brother Geoffrey standing alone, looking through the grand wall-to-ceiling windows of the hall at the blizzard roaring outside. Even in the reflection I could see his brows furrowed, like fuzzy red caterpillars mating, just as they had been in the room below the library when our guest revealed his name. He had made some small conversation with a few folk but chose to be introverted, which did not suit a man of his stature in the least.

I wanted to find out what was souring the monk's mood, so I excused myself from the physician and went to his side; we watched in quiet unison as the curtain of snow descended upon the stage of the Whitaker House's grounds.

"You suddenly seem a bit short on conversation," I remarked. "Is what we discussed earlier troubling you?"

He pulled at his abundant beard before speaking. "Obviously, the undertones to this merry occasion have me a bit glum."

"You have that same look about you that you wore when you pushed our host to pinpoint his place of origin. I could tell then that you weren't pleased with his generality."

"It's not so much that," the friar replied. "Many people that immigrate are reluctant to talk about their homeland, for most times they are fleeing war, famine, and persecution."

"What then?" I persisted.

The ample monk sighed and, once more, he squinted out into the waves of blowing snow. He then posited, "When was the last time you observed a snow storm of this veracity?"

Expecting this to be a circumlocution, I answered, as I studied the white torrent on the other side of the glass, "I'm not sure I've ever seen a wintery display as magnificent as this."

"Nor I," he returned.

I only stared at him with brow askew. I did not have to ask again. I could tell he was about to let me in on some revelation.

Suddenly, there was a hand at my back, tugging on my shirt. I turned to see one of the children, a pretty auburn haired girl, with a red gift in her hand. "Sir," she asked, "could you help me put this on the Christmas tree?" She then turned and pointed to a bare tree branch about six feet up.

I smiled and agreed.

"I'll be right back," I said.

"And I'll shall be here," Brother Geoffrey replied dryly, never taking his focus off the storm outside.

Within a few minutes, I returned to find Mr. Willoughby, a local merchant, asking the whereabouts of our host. It seemed he had left the room. Upon further inspection, it seemed his two associates were missing, as well.

"I guess I will have to thank him at a later date," Mr. Willoughby said. "For I live on the other side of the village, and I fear it will be all I can do just to make it home in such weather. I must leave now before the walk becomes impassable."

I looked around, as the other guests were, themselves, becoming ill at ease with the growing storm.

"It looks as though the timing of this dinner was a bit off," I said, as I surveyed the room of worry-grown faces.

"Not necessarily," Brother Geoffrey said under his breath, as Mr. Willoughby joined some of the other adults at the large fireplace.

"Now what does that mean?" I worriedly asked. "Tell me, man, what it is that has got you so up in arms about this foreigner."

"It's his name," the big Scotsman uttered with a slight quiver in his voice.

"Victor Strigoi? What about it makes you this way?"

"Its meaning. It means..." He paused a moment. "His last name, Strigoi — in the region he comes from, it means *undead*. It is not our host who need fear of dying prematurely. It is one of us here, and I fear it will happen this very night."

Just as he uttered that statement, Mr. Strigoi, along with his two associates, re-entered the hall. "I see by the look on your faces," he began with that deep resonant tone, "that you fear returning to your homes this evening because of the storm."

A chorus in the affirmative echoed around the hall.

"Please, I would hate to have this wonderful evening end abruptly because of Mother Nature's — inhospitality. I have made arrangements to have rooms set up for each of you. You can spend the night as my guests and leave when the storm abates."

When everyone agreed to the hospitality, a smile stretched from under his neatly trimmed mustache. However, when he turned to the two of us at the windows, his smile turned devilish. "Will the two of you stay and grace my company, as well?"

I can only assume the monk decided to stay because, as a man of God, he could not back down from the Prince of Darkness.

As for myself I, too, lived quite a walk away. I was beginning to fear the man but feared the storm more. I decided to risk my fate at the Whitaker House with Brother Geoffrey's sizable bulk at my side, than to surely die of exposure on such a treacherous walk home.

Please excuse me; I do not mean to pull you from the story, as I remember it. But it is nearly midnight, and I now hear movement from within my home. It is the kind of slow, deliberate activity that sets blood to chill, like a bully pounding his fist in the palm of his hand when the object of his torment is cornered.

The Evil One is here, and he has begun his search. He may soon be at my door. I haven't yet taken any precautions to delay his entry into my room, so I must do so now and lock and barricade my door. I know it is a trifling task, for the strongest steel and thickest oak could not stop him, who is evil and eternal. But fear dictates action, however frivolous it may seem. I can only hope that I will be able to finish the story I've started.

3

I apologize for my absence, though whoever reads these words at some later time will not know an absence was taken except by my admission. The intruder is gaining ground but not yet ready to take me, so I will pick up on this horrific tale where I had previously left off.

Our host came and went as the evening progressed. He entertained with stories during dinner, which had all but Brother Geoffrey mesmerized, then left during an impromptu chorus of Christmas carols sung by the children. Later, he would materialize again with his two associates, make rounds, saying his 'how do you do's', then leave once more. No one seemed to care of his comings and goings. They must have assumed that he had probably brought home a particular worrisome case in which he was preoccupied and was doing a remarkable job of balancing his duties as host and a busy lawyer.

The big red monk thought otherwise and convinced me of the same.

"When the others are occupied by the fireside," he told me in a forced whisper, "I am going to slip out and try to find out what endeavors our host is occupied in while not in our company. Come with me. There is strength in numbers."

I agreed, though in my heart I was fearful. The place and its new owner were taxing my lucidity by the second.

When everyone — including some of the servants — had gathered around the large hearth to tell Christmas stories, the monk and I stole from the room surreptitiously. The banquet hall opened up into an expansive, empty hall, which is where we then stood, pondering our next course of action.

The place was silent outside the hall, save the ghoulish shriek at our backs from the storm winds breaching a cracked stained glass window that had yet been mended.

"Where shall we look for Mr. Strigoi? The house is so large, and he could be anywhere."

Brother Geoffrey replied, "Whatever devilish things he may be up to would have to be done away from the notice of the guests. I suggest we start our search upstairs."

He hurried down the wide hall towards the front of the house as I followed behind. There, to the right of the immense front entranceway, was a glorious marble staircase the color of jade. We took only a moment's hesitation to eye one another fearfully before slowly walking up the stairs side by side.

At the top of the staircase, centered on the wall of the landing, was a large window overlooking the frozen gardens below that separated Whitaker House from the desolate moor, beyond. From there, the stairs spiraled up to a third floor, or you could follow the landing around to the right to a long corridor lined with many doors.

But it was that window that had caught our collective eye; a crimson glow spilled a most diabolical color onto the falling torrents, as if a great fire raged amidst the snow and ice.

We both rushed to the glass to investigate the eerie light's origin.

I cupped my hands around my eyes and searched for an earthly cause but found none.

Brother Geoffrey turned his attention skyward and found the source; one floor above us, in the south wing, a brilliant light was cascading from the window of one of the rooms. We both could see great columns of steam rising from the pane, as tides of snow were driven onto the glass only to be instantly melted away.

If I had any lingering reservations about the monk's intimations regarding our host, they left me in a sudden gasp of horror.

"We must try our best to beat the evil prince at his own game," Brother Geoffrey said as he made the sign of the cross.

Before I had time to form any rebuttal, we were off again, climbing the great green staircase one more floor. This floor was laid out the same as the previous one, except the staircase ended; there were no other floors beyond this one.

We crept down the long corridor until we found the one occupied. Rays of red light, like that given off by a great bonfire, slipped out from under the door and through the keyhole. I touched the door but immediately withdrew my hand, for the heat was unbearable. I could not help but wonder why the door hadn't yet caught fire, but by this time

I had stopped asking questions about the supernatural event that was transpiring before my very eyes.

Suddenly, the doorknob slowly turned.

My eyes widened at the thought of what lay beyond the door, and the thread that held my sanity finally broke. I ran yelling for my very life back down the corridor towards the stairs, while Brother Geoffrey pursued, insisting we face the Prince of Darkness together.

"I can't do it!" I protested. "I don't have the faith needed to fight such a fallen angel."

"Where two or more of us are gathered together…" the monk replied, quoting familiar scripture. "God is with us, Mr. Croft. Who can be against us?"

Continuing to the staircase I said, "Comforting words will not suffice. I wish to leave this place and take my chances with the snow. We all must leave. If we go in a group, we can go to the nearest home and stay there till the storm passes. At any rate, I will not stay a moment longer."

"Help me!" he insisted.

"I will not, I cannot!" I exclaimed.

I proved to be a bit quicker than my portly pursuer, but he followed close behind. I never bothered to look back at who—or what—opened the door to the room. I only carried myself in haste to what I had assumed was the safety of the group of people still telling Christmas stories in the banquet hall two floors below.

Suddenly, as I made the top of the stairs, readying myself for a quick descent, one of Mr. Strigoi's associates almost ran into me, as he was making his way up. His abrupt appearance and our near collision startled me even more.

As I stopped and turned back to avoid colliding with him, the friar came up from behind me. In my avoidance of one collision another ensued. Brother Geoffrey lost his ample balance and spilled down the marble stairs with a yelp. On his second of many rolls, his head made contact with the cold marble, and he let out a winded sigh that quickly abated. When his body tumbled to a rest at the landing of the next floor down, a small pool of blood formed round about his head.

"My heavens!" I blurted breathlessly. "What have I done? Oh, what have I done?"

With a look of concern, Mr. Strigoi's associate said, "I was on my way to my room when I heard what I thought was quarreling, so I came up to investigate."

Walking with cane in hand, and dressed now in a long red robe that covered nightwear, Mr. Strigoi appeared in the corridor from which I had just abruptly excused myself. "What's going on here?" he asked. "I had heard some noises outside my bedroom door and as I opened it, I heard screaming and pleading of some sort."

We all looked down on the monk's lifeless body for just a moment before Mr. Strigoi's associate turned to me. "What had he done to you that would cause you to do this?"

I could only blink in disbelief; shock seems to have a way of draining the life even out of the living.

"Mr. Croft, did you do this?" Mr. Strigoi asked.

"I saw the whole thing," his associate said. "Though I don't know his intentions, to me it looked as though Mr. Croft pushed him down the stairs."

Finally, I exclaimed, "No, it was an accident, I assure you. An accident!"

Mr. Strigoi rubbed his manicured beard thoughtfully then looked out the landing window. "It seems the storm has momentarily abated."

I turned and inspected the window, as well. It was true. As suddenly as the storm had begun, it vanished. The stars could even be seen twinkling in the night sky beyond the glass.

"The constable's house is only a few blocks away," he continued. "As a lawyer, I must keep this scene just the way it is and keep all parties separated until the authorities arrive. Barabus, go retrieve Dr. McGinty from the banquet hall then retire to your bedroom and speak to no one until the authorities arrive. Mr. Croft, come with me, and I will dispatch my other associate to retrieve the constable."

After all the details were taken care of, I followed Mr. Strigoi back to his bedroom.

"May I ask what the two of you were doing outside my room?" he asked as we slowly made our way back down the hallway.

I felt embarrassed but decided to tell him truthfully of the house's curse and who the dead Brother Geoffrey thought he really was.

He laughed aloud when I had finished. "Come, I will show you what nefarious lights were burning from within my room."

The great heated light turned out to be a mammoth fireplace that churned out the largest fire I had ever seen inside a home.

"The red glow you saw," Mr. Strigoi said, "was probably the firelight filtered through my silk robe as I paced around the room."

Even as he spoke, perspiration broke out on my forehead and trickled down my face. "How can you stand such heat?" I queried as I pulled out a handkerchief and wiped my face clean.

"I have a skin condition that worsens in winter time due to the dryness of cold air. One of the reasons why I moved here was because of the usually moist but rarely frozen winters. When it started to snow and the temperature dropped, my skin began to break out in a rash, which is why I could not stay in your company long. Perspiration, oddly enough, lessens the condition, so I had a large fire built to keep me from scratching myself into oblivion. I have had this for as long as I can remember. I can only assume my tolerance to heat is somewhat more than the average person's."

I pondered his explanation for a moment then couldn't help but smile. It seemed as though that I had been so caught up in Brother Geoffrey's tale that all rationale had left me. There had been a sensible explanation to all the night's happenings if they had been but given a chance to take form.

"But what about your name?" I asked dutifully, making sure I left nothing to chance. "Brother Geoffrey said it meant 'undead' in your native tongue."

"Is not the name Miller given to someone who may not necessarily be a miller? And Baker given to a one who may not be a baker? And Archer given to a person who may never have picked up a bow in his life?"

I nodded in agreement and felt a bit foolish.

"If I were you," he then added, "There are much more troubling things about which to worry at the moment."

My heart sank as I pondered the monk, whose death, though an accident, was at my hands. "What must I do? What will happen next? It was an accident. While trying to avoid colliding with your associate, the monk and I got tangled, and that, not anger, precipitated his fall."

The man went to a steamer trunk that was still packed but open on a chair next to his bed. From there, he withdrew a document and motioned me to him.

"If you wish, I can represent you. You will need council on your end, if this matter is to be resolved."

"You do believe it was an accident, then?" I asked, hopeful.

He smiled oddly and said, "If I didn't then I would not have offered my services."

"What must I do?"

"Sign here on this document, and I will represent you as your legal counsel. I do not think I have to remind you that the only witness to this *accident* seems to think he heard an argument before the dreadful event. That does not bode well for your defense. But I can say with honesty that I am the best at what I do."

He said the last statement with a knowing smile and devilish glint in his eye that I was too fearful at the time to recognize.

I replied, "But I am a man of relatively meager earnings. How could I afford a lawyer of your caliber?"

"Do not worry about recompense for the moment. I feel terrible enough that this unfortunance has happened within my home. I can assure you that my services will not cost you what you cannot relinquish. Just sign on the dotted line."

He offered me a pen, which I took in hand and looked down at the old parchment. "It seems to be written in a foreign language. What does it say?"

Mr. Strigoi smiled sheepishly. "I apologize. I am fresh from my home country, and this is the only document I have on hand. I can assure you of its authenticity. Even though written in my dialect, it will stand up legally in your court system. It is just a matter of translation when the time comes. Please, sign here and let me help you. I can assure you that you will not go to jail for this. It is my word. I guarantee my word."

Beginning to get uneasy about the possible ramifications of this terrible accident, and at last believing that the lawyer could save me, I signed.

Suddenly, that devilish grin re-appeared on his face, more severe in its creases, as the skin around his cheeks piled in crimson waves. When he spoke again, it was as though that great bass voice dropped an octave, but even then I had no idea what had just transpired.

"Follow me," he said in a frighteningly deliberate tone.

I followed him back to the top of the stairs and looked down upon Brother Geoffrey leaning up against the railing, feeling the back of his head. His great bulk rested wobbly on his feet, but he seemed none the worse for wear.

Brother Geoffrey, you are alive!"

"Alive but not well," he said groggily, as he examined the blood on his retrieved hand. "I must go and see the doctor and leave this place. You would be well advised, Mr. Croft, to do the same."

With that, the friar stumbled down the stairs to the entranceway below.

I smiled at Mr. Strigoi. "I thank you, sir, but it looks as though I will not be needing your services."

"Ah, but my services have already been rendered."

I turned and pointed down the stairs. "But what services have you rendered? Didn't you see? The monk was not killed in the fall."

His grin had by this time turned into an impossibly grander smile. "Yes, my dear Mr. Croft, he was most certainly dead. However, you cannot be tried for murder if the deceased gets up and walks away — that was my service to you."

As he turned his back to me and began walking away, he said without looking back, "And I will be back in exactly one year to collect my fee."

It was at this moment that I knew without a doubt with whom I was dealing. As I pondered my fate in the fires of the netherworld, I silently watched him walk slowly back down the corridor to his blood colored room. I am certain that, as I watched, his faint footsteps turned into the clapping of hooves upon the wooden floor.

And it is that same sound I now hear outside my bedroom door. My heart now pounds so heavily that it threatens to break free of my chest. He is here! The knob on my bedroom door is turning. The Devil has come to ta —

I'm Still Alive

1

Doctor Arless slowly descended the stairs, wiping a restless sleep from his eyes. Sleep, as well as sanity, seemed to leech from his pores nightly, until day upon day of the last six months molded into one hazy, waking nightmare.

At the bottom of the stairs, he stretched his tired limbs and yawned—his body's failed attempt to force upon itself an energy for the day it did not at the moment have, nay seemed to have an exquisite aversion to.

He blinked into focus the once warmly decorated foyer around him festooned with flowery accents, lace, and polished surfaces. A large mahogany grandfather clock ticked softly against the wall, and an oval, stained glass window spilled a kaleidoscope of colors across the entranceway from its perch above the front door; they were now but ornamental scabs that covered a deep and festering wound.

To the right of the entranceway was the broad archway to the living room and the dining room beyond, no doubt already set with a cold breakfast, which their housekeeper, Olivia, faithfully put out each morning before going to market. The habit of eight years prevented her from setting less than two places at the table, yet only one was needed, had only been needed for some time.

He hesitated only briefly before finally casting his weary gaze to the closed door on the opposite wall, clenching and rubbing his hands, as if unsure what to do with them. Finally, he settled on burying them in his housecoat pockets.

One long sigh later he was at the door.

This was once a sitting room. Now it was a dying room.

He gently turned the cold, brass knob, hesitated, then opened the door and disappeared inside, feeling as though he was but morsel being forced down the gullet of Death itself.

Laying in the bed, covers pulled and tucked up to her neck, was Mrs. Arless — the reason for his unstable mind these past months. She looked even paler than usual, with dark rings round about her eyes. Small, weeping pustules dotted her forehead and settled cheeks. Her breathing was shallow and stuttered.

She mustn't have heard him enter the room, for she never wrestled from under her covering, eyes never flittered from under their gray lids. It was still early, and she was rarely conscious for more than a few hours a day, anymore.

Her labored breaths made her husband pull in deep breaths of stale air reflexively, as though he too found it difficult to breath.

In taxing his lung capacity while listening to his wife labor to fill her own chest, he realized she hadn't soiled herself in the night. Good. He hated cleaning up after her when she had, usually leaving that task to Olivia. With his housemaid at market, it would have been an unavoidable, if not malodorous, condition in which to leave her until Olivia returned.

Dr. Arless slowly approached her bed and tried to look upon her with the same affection and sympathy he'd had for her in the early stages of her illness. However, all he could now muster was a cold apathy that daily grew ever closer to a full-blown odium.

The reason for this slow but steady degradation was a simple if not narcissistic one: At one time, not that many months prior, he and his were the epitome of style, grace, and beauty. Everyone loved them, respected them, envied them.

Now, however, when he looked upon his patients and walked the streets of Halverton-Upon-Dees, he could see the pitiful stares. Their expressions may have meant to convey sympathy, but in his eyes they were stares of disdain, disgust — *How could this have happened to the Arless's? He's is a doctor; why can't he make her better?* — As though that profession somehow precluded one from being affected by disease, maybe even death itself, knowing the mental capacity for superstition rampant in this village.

Being a physician, however, this "noble profession" was only a hobby, really — the way some approached botany or lepidoptery. His true calling was helping his wife spend her money, an occupation for which he was truly born and dutifully undertook. They were not nobility but were well off enough financially to run in upper circles, even if running meant the shoving of some shoulders and jockeying for a position they might not otherwise have, if not for the effort of attaining it. And certainly, being a physician had helped to forge friendships that would otherwise have been off limits to them.

Now, however, he who regularly graced the Coliseum Opera, spent many an afternoon fox hunting with Sir Audley at his estate in Oxford, and frequently spent holiday on the continent, no longer found time for these fancies; when not seeing other patients, his day was consumed with his ill wife's care. He wished with all his might that this burden would be taken from him, but daily she suffered, and daily he suffered more still.

She lay as still as death itself, save for the slight rise and fall of her chest. He stared for a long while, motionless, watching with open eyes and closed heart. At one point, his hand started towards her snarled and lubricious hair in an unconscious movement to push that matted mess from her eyes. Yet before his hand could accomplish its task, he jerked it back suddenly, as if touching her would seal upon him the same sickening fate.

The room was moist in the warm August morning and oddly quiet. Although larks sang hidden in the wheat field, which separated their parcel and the priory at the top of the hill beyond; and although their song was borne on a gentle breeze that ruffled the curtains at the far end of the room, the doctor neither heard nor noticed any of it.

He seemed deaf, now, to any and all splendor.

At once, the body under the covers began to stir, slowly at first. Heavy, crusted eyes blinked open, and her cracked lips stretched to a weak smile, as her gaze fell upon her husband.

There in that place, a malevolence, which had slowly taken root in the oft shadowed corners of the room like a dark weed, found a crack in the soul of that man and entered — as weeds are wont to do — into a place it did not belong. A blackness that had been held at arm's length for so long finally found embrace in the most unlikely of people — a physician, a husband.

He returned a feeble smile and leaned over his wife in an embrace yet immediately retracted with a pillow, her head briefly bouncing off the bed underneath. Her eyes blinked in confusion at first, then suddenly widened in fear, as the pillow was pressed down over her face with vice-like force.

His wife, with what little strength remained, tried desperately to get out from under his grasp, screaming as best as her failing body would allow. Those muffled screams of terror, however, were trapped in a web of down, barely audible to the ears on the other side.

It seemed the harder she fought, the quicker she slackened. The woman tried in feeble desperation to free her hands from under the silken covers to fight the devil disguised as her salvation, however they were stretched tight over her body, making the simple task difficult even for an escape artist.

The dark deed was done in less than two minutes. It was surprisingly easy, yet catching his breath was difficult, and the doctor's heart thumped like a drum in his chest.

After wiping cold beads of sweat from his forehead and drying the dampness on his housecoat, Dr. Arless replaced the pillow under her slackened neck, first turning the ooze- and saliva-stained side down, away from any questioning eyes. He then pressed and tucked the disheveled bedding back into its creaseless perfection, as smooth as a pond on a windless day.

He looked down on his beloved's lifeless body. The newly *late* Mrs. Arless looked quite peaceful. More at rest than she had been for months.

A tear trickled down his cheek, which he promptly wiped away. In the forest of his heart, it was the last falling leaf from a tree reluctant to cede the warmth and sun of summer to the cold, dark, barren winter.

Yet winter came to him, nonetheless, and with a vengeance.

At last, a shadow of a smile creased the edges of his mouth.

Dr. Arless finally let out a long sigh of exhilaration, turned, and went back upstairs to get ready for his day.

2

The doctor was looping his tie around his neck when he heard the scream. Olivia had been home for fifteen minutes; he was surprised he hadn't heard the exclamation sooner.

"Sir!" she screamed from the bottom of the stairs.

The doctor appeared at the top finishing his tie.

The young lady was ashen faced and breathing heavily. At that rate, he knew, her corset would prevent her from receiving enough air, and she would soon faint if he didn't calm her down.

"The missus...I think...She's..." She couldn't finish her sentence and ran back into the room.

"For god's sake, woman," he said under his breath, as he descended the stairs, "what on earth did you expect the eventual outcome to be?"

When Dr. Arless finally entered the room, Olivia was standing next to the bed sobbing. She turned to him with tears in her eyes. "She's dead, sir. She must have passed after I went to market. I looked in on her before I left. Oh, I should never have left her."

He put a reassuring hand on her shoulder then passed by her to look over his work. The doctor felt for a pulse but couldn't feel one, didn't expect one. His wife was still warm, however that was probably due to her being under the covers and the warming morning.

He sighed. "Rest in peace my dear."

He then turned to Olivia. "I hate to ask this of you, but would you be a dear go over to the priory and have the vicar come by at once. Then go to the village and fetch Chief Constable Bowers and Mr. Timmons."

"Mr. Timmons?"

"He is the executer of Gwen's will."

"Pardon my asking, sir, but why do we need him at this point?"

Dr. Arless put his arm around her and led Olivia out of the room. "Because in her will, Gwen lays out how she wants her remains to be treated."

"Oh," she said knowingly. "Because of her—".

"Yes," he replied cutting her off. "Now, go. I'll change into my mourning clothes, get the house in order, and sit with her till you return. Protocol, my dear. Protocol."

. . . .

All was quiet. Olivia had been gone a half hour. Depending at which of his daily tasks she found him, the vicar should be arriving at any moment.

The doctor had donned the traditional black suit with a black band around his left arm, carried out the customary traditions of stopping the clock at the time of death, covered the mirrors, and drew the curtains in every room.

He now sat at her bedside wiping his forehead with a black handkerchief; the day was warming quite nicely and with the curtains drawn, no breeze could bypass the thick, velvet curtains.

He smiled a genuine smile at her, as he pulled and primped absentmindedly at her sheets. The relief he felt was monumental. Now he could get on with his life after the proper amount of mourning. The grieving time was an inconvenience he would be happy to endure to free his life from the burden of her care.

He closed his eyes, imagining the blissful times that lie ahead, times he sorely missed.

However, when he opened them back up, his heart leapt into his throat when his wife's own eyes opened, and she engaged him directly with a slight bend of her neck, the way a dog cocks its head when it hears an odd sound. Her cold, dead stare sent a snake of ice slithering down his back.

She opened her mouth, at which time a tiny rivulet of blood trickled from its corner. Her voice sounded like broken machinery when she said, "I'm still alive." She smiled a devilish smile at him and in the blink of an eye, her arms were released from their silken bondage, and she was reaching out for him with emaciated limbs that scrabbled wildly for his neck.

The doctor fell backwards out of his chair with a *thud* to escape her death grip and let out a quiet yelp, as he stumbled over himself to reach the bedroom door. His terror was as palpable as the heat in the room, and he felt the blood drain from his face, as though bleeding out from an unseen wound.

Once at the door, he quickly staggered to his feet, sure that she was right behind him but unsure from where her sudden reanimation came. The room behind him hung in a sepulchral darkness, save for a sliver of late summer sun that flashed from between the heavy curtains, striking the contours on the bed.

He flung open the heavy oak, flooding the room with harsh light and noticed from the corner of his eye the body of his dead wife, still board-stiff, eyes closed, under her bedding. The light made her look like a wax figure on the verge of melting.

He engaged her once more, albeit apprehensively, from the doorway, wiping a cold sweat from his neck, trying desperately to calm his piston pounding heart. She was still dead, hadn't moved, hadn't opened her eyes, hadn't said those terrible words.

His wide eyes slackened, and finally he laughed. It was a phantasm of his mind. He must have dozed off sitting in his chair, and the ghostly encounter was a revenant of his subconscious.

The doctor pulled out his pocket watch with a still shaking hand; the vicar should be arriving momentarily and a bit later, Olivia et al. He calmly smoothed out the wrinkles from his suit coat, pushed back into place his disheveled, black hair, and returned to his mourning station beside Gwen Arless's bed — after pulling back the chair to a more suitable distance.

In Victorian society, there was a proper way to do everything. He killed her properly; now he had to mourn her properly. That is what society demanded, and he was a child of society.

3

Surprisingly, those summoned all arrived together. Olivia led them through the door, each wearing an uncomfortable mask of commiseration. Each shook Dr. Arless's hand and offered condolences.

He, in turn, offered them Mrs. Arless's room with a sweep of his arm.

Olivia whispered to the doctor as they entered together, "Vicar was in town, sir. I hope you don't mind them all at once."

"Not at all, Olivia," he lied. "I quite needed the time to myself."

Each stood quietly for a moment looking upon the body.

The vicar broke the silence. "She looks so much more at peace now than since the last time I looked in on her. She's in a better place now."

All the guests nodded solemnly. The doctor, however, did not ascent. He stood motionless, as if he didn't even hear the old cleric speak.

Finally, Constable Bowers uncurled his tall frame, straightening out the revere of his uniform. "Well, doctor," he said as he cleared his throat and started looking over the body, the bed, and the room, "all seems to be in order. Nothing suspicious jumps out at me — not that I expected anything, you see. Everyone knew of Mrs. Arless's illness. All this is just a formality, of course."

"Of course," replied Arless dryly. "That is why I had Olivia summon you."

The officer pulled out a small pad and a pencil and wrote down some notes. "Olivia explained everything to us on the way here. I'll just jot it down and be on my way. Paperwork, you know."

After a moment of scribbling, Bowers put his pad away and turned to leave. Before walking through the door, he turned and put an uncomfortable hand on the doctor's shoulder. "Very sorry for you loss, doctor."

He turned and left.

Mr. Timmons turned to Dr. Arless, satchel in hand, and whispered, "Are you ready?"

"I'm quite sure I know what's in it, but let's make it official."

The vicar gave them a reverent look and began a whispered prayer as he pulled a glass trinket filled with fragrant oil and a Bible from a black leather purse.

The doctor looked upon the old man with incredulity. He was a High Anglican, more Catholic than Protestant, but neither lie appealed to him. Gwen, on the other hand was devout and considered Vicar Pratt a friend. She had managed to gain her husband entrance to a church service on but a few occasions, which he found both dull and given to extreme melancholy. His mind always wandered to more festive destinations than those two in the afterlife always mentioned in the vicar's sermons, both of which he was certain did not exist.

"Olivia, could you get some tea on for us please?" he asked.

Olivia nodded, curtsied slightly then left the room to attend her task.

"Let's go into the parlor," he said to Timmons.

As they exited the room, Timmons turned his head and mentioned over his shoulder, "Vicar, this involves you, as well. Do what you need to do here. We will wait for you to join us then begin."

. . . .

Mr. Timmons settled his rotund fixtures into a green velvet settee with his well-worn satchel on his lap. He released its leather straps and meticulously placed the papers from within it onto a small, oval rosewood table straddled between himself and a leather wing-back chair, which Dr. Arless occupied. The lawyer's eyes gleamed behind his pince-nez glasses at his perfectly aligned paperwork the way a man might pour over the sparsely clad contents of a brothel.

Although the doctor saw no such blemish, Timmons must have seen a corner slightly askew, for he suddenly reached over his ample lap and began to rearrange them yet again.

He was about this task when Olivia entered with a tray of tea. So much did it tremble in her hands that she threatened to rain the fragrant contents onto the paperwork, table, and plush carpet underneath, which would have been tantamount to murder in the eyes of the barrister.

Dr. Arless quickly grabbed the silver from her and gently placed it on the table, pouring then handing a cup of tea to Timmons and taking one himself. "Thank you, Olivia. That will be all. I'll ring if I need anything else."

Forgetting her curtsy, the young woman just turned and walked quickly from the room, wiping a flood of tears from her cheeks.

The vicar entered shortly after and grabbed a small, armless chair from the corner and took his seat between the two men around the table.

The vicar eyed the tea momentarily, but when none was immediately offered, he fixed his gaze between the doctor and the lawyer, and his was a queer expression.

Dr. Arless noticed. "Is everything alright?"

"Yes, yes," he said, his voice trailing off. After a moment, "It's just that when I was anointing her with oil, she seemed...she was still very warm."

Understanding what the statement implied, the doctor replied, "I assure you vicar, she is dead. No pulse, no breath. That means dead."

"Yes, yes, far be it from me to question you —"

"Then don't," Dr. Arless rejoined with a controlled exasperation.

"It's just…she is still very warm, considering she's been passed some two or more hours. Very unusual."

"It's the end of August, on what seems to be turning out to be one of the warmest days of the summer. The curtains are drawn and the door to her room is closed. Just what would you expect?"

Mr. Timmons interjected himself between the two. "This is precisely why we need to have this conversation. May we put our anger in check and begin."

"Of course," replied the vicar. "I apologize for my remarks. They weren't meant to offend. They were just the ramblings of an old man holding onto the hope of a dear friend." Eyeing them both he then said, "I must say, though, I am curious as to why I must be part of this."

Regaining composure himself, Dr. Arless ignored the vicar's apology and nodded for Mr. Timmons to begin.

"Well, as you may know, John," nodding to Dr. Arless, "and may not know," nodding in turn to Vicar Pratt, "Mrs. Arless was given to certain — peculiar proclivities."

At this, the doctor nodded agreeably, and the vicar turned a twisted brow at the lawyer.

"So we all understand and are not at cross purposes I will explain." He repositioned his pince-nez farther up his nose and began, "Just over six years ago, Mrs. Arless, Gwen, lost her brother William to Typhoid. All thought he had expired, indeed, all indications were that he had. However, just as he was being preserved for burial with arsenic, he miraculously revived, only to die genuinely from the preserving fluid already injected into his veins."

At this, the vicar let out a mew of astonishment, and Dr. Arless sighed in quiet exasperation at the vicar.

Continuing, Mr. Timmons said, "From that point on Gwen has had a great fear of death — or more precisely stated, a fear of not actually being dead."

"Seems she and the vicar are of one mind on this," the doctor replied phlegmatically, as he sipped his tea.

Both the vicar and the lawyer ignored the retort.

"I believe we all know that Gwen's family is one of some means. Knowing her fear, rational or not, they procured for her a special casket. This casket is fitted with tubing to allow fresh air into the casket and a rope that leads from within the casket to a bell affixed above ground, which she can pull should she revive after burial."

"I had no idea she had such an extreme anxiety over such a thing," replied the vicar.

"It wasn't a detail she wished to share with many people for understandable reasons," said Dr. Arless.

"So now we come to the particulars," Mr. Timmons expounded. "Gwen did not wish to be preserved."

The vicar's face reddened. "What? No preservation? We need at least three days to plan the funeral and service, send out invitations. In this weather, she'll be...well, unfit for viewing within a day."

"Precisely," said Timmons. "That is why she is going to be buried this evening."

"This is most unusual. Are you in accordance with this, Dr. Arless?"

He only shrugged his shoulders as he poured himself another cup of tea. After tasting it and gently placing a second sugar cube in the hot liquid, he finally said, feigning sadness, "It is too bad that it has come to this, however these are my dear Gwen's wishes, and I was nothing if not a slave to her happiness." Inwardly, however, his only sadness was that the opportunity for a grand celebration to send Gwen off to her reward would be wasted.

"We are to prepare her for burial here. I have already sent for the casket, which should arrive late this afternoon from Wellerby's in Oxford. We will have a small service here with a small contingent of friends, which she has already laid out. She will be buried in the church yard, and someone will stand guard overnight in case she should revive and ring the bell. In that case, a hasty un-burial will ensue. Now, if there is no revival by mid-day tomorrow, per her request, we may disconnect the tubing and bell from Mrs. Arless's casket and begin our mourning properly."

Mr. Timmons engaged Dr. Arless directly. "Do you think Olivia would be willing to dress her for burial?"

"No. She is a mess. She was barely able to bring tea. It will have to be someone else."

"The missus has done this many a time," interjected Vicar Pratt. "If you have a dress picked out I'm sure she and our Molly would be honored to do it for you."

"Is that agreeable to you, John?"

"It isn't the scenario I envisioned."

"I doubt any of this is."

He turned to the reverend. "That will be fine. Thank you." It was a hard sentence to say. It felt coming out like food stuck in his windpipe. But it had to be done. He didn't wish for her body to linger in the house and above ground any longer than it had to.

"It's settled then," Timmons said. "With some signatures, we can get this somber endeavor underway."

And the vicar replied, "May she rest in peace."

Dr. Arless said nothing as he finished his tea.

4

Within an hour, Mrs. Pratt and her servant Molly arrived. They cordially dispensed with the usual solemnities then set about their task of transforming the dead to look alive once more. Dr. Arless gave them the burial dress, and Olivia provided accompanying accoutrements she and Mrs. Arless had, with much reluctance and crying, picked out in the early stages of her illness.

As the vicar's wife closed the door to Gwen's room, the doctor suddenly found himself with nothing to do. He decided to take in a walk; after all it was a fine summer day without rain, and it was well past noon without, as yet, so much as a step outside.

Being without the confines of that dreadful room, and having his soul lifted from the release of a burden that nearly suffocated his happiness, beauty somehow found its way back to him. The sky was bathed in blue, a sea in the heavens that matched any on earth. Clouds, like mighty galleons marched along the horizon, off to lands distant. Throngs of golden wheat swayed in hypnotic unison to a song more whispered than sung on the late summer breezes, and the serried tops of beech, oak, and elm trees swooned like sozzled sentries between all the properties.

All this he took in with great pleasure, as he ambled along.

The physician followed one of the wooded delineations that separated the wheat field from the parsonage down a gentle slope and inside of a ten minute walk, he was at the River Dees. Wide swatches of green grass were patched together by majestic weeping willows along its banks.

Under one of these trees was a lone fisherman, his pole propped on a stick, his line swallowed by the sky-mirrored currents. He stood, his back to the doctor, pike stiff, as if any sudden movement would scare any potential fish — and probably his supper — away.

The doctor was not much in the mood for conversation. However, he saw no way out of the inevitability, considering they were the only two at the river, and he refused to try a stealthy retreat and possibly embarrass himself if caught. Just a quick *hello* and *any luck yet?*, and he would be on his way down the well-worn path, contemplating life without his Gwen.

Dr. Arless leadened his steps so as not to startle the man, as he came up from behind and called out, "Hullo. How's the endeavor panning out so far?"

The man never moved, gave no indication that he had even heard the salutation.

As the doctor came shoulder to shoulder with the man, he surveyed the water and said again, "I say, have you had any luck yet?"

The man finally engaged him directly, but the shock of what he saw sent the doctor stumbling backwards in terror; it was the face of his dead wife engaging him, hair a tangle of worms and matted mud, nostrils infested with wriggling masses of maggots, cheeks pocked with curdled divots, more bone than flesh. Gwen Arless looked as though she had been the main course at a carrion feast. The doctor was saved from having to engage her with direct eye contact for she had none. Where her beautiful sapphires had been in life (they were by far her most pronounced attribute) were now but hollow sockets with wasting cerebral contents faintly seen in the shadows beneath. That face of death smiled, and it was a smile that was sour with rot.

"I'm still alive," her flaking lips uttered in a vomitous clatter.

As he stumbled back, the doctor's foot slipped off the path, and his spill backwards turned into a waste deep bath in a cold river.

The fisherman from hell jumped from the bank into the murky water with Dr. Arless, closing the distance between the two in the blink of an eye. The doctor pushed himself backwards in the cool currents, trying to keep distance between himself and the man who wore his wife's decayed face. Water splashed in high arcs and digested in slobbery coughs as two hands reached out for his throat. Death's grasp was steel-strong, rough, cold.

"Dr.! Dr. Arless, you alright?"

Suddenly, Mrs. Arless's face was replaced with one more deserving of a living body. It was Sean Caudill, one of the local farm hands. "Didn't mean t'scare ya like'at," he said in his slow, Cornish burr. "Didn't hear ye come up behind me. Guess I was just lost'n me own thoughts, I was."

He reached out a hand to Dr. Arless.

The doctor hesitated momentarily, making sure the hand being offered did not show bone and sinew before being helped up.

A moment later, they had made their way up the bank and back onto the path.

Both men looked like soggy loaves of bread laying on the sun-dappled path, each trying to catch their breath and wringing river water from their clothes.

"I'm s'sorry, Dr. Arless," Sean pleaded once again, wiping his wet, sandy hair from his eyes. "I ne'er meant fer that t'happen."

Panting through a heavy, matted mess of saturated clothing, the doctor waved off the comment and looked over his pathetic, dripping visage. However, his sodden attire was not foremost on mind. The picture of his dead wife was still emblazoned before him, and her words still felt like hat pins thrust into his ears. Her spirit was taunting him. But he didn't believe in the afterlife, did he? Her dead body had somehow become manifest in the countenance of others. But how? Why?

A shiver coursed his body, not entirely due to his cold, wet clothes.

After only a moment, the young farm hand noticed the black band on Dr. Arless's coat sleeve. "I'm sorry f'yer loss, sir," he said nodding at the band. "Lot a us bin prayin' hard fer the missus (at this he made a sign of the cross, to which Dr. Arless did his best not to roll his eyes). Help't us when she could, she did. When d'it happen?"

"Just this morning. The vicar's wife was so kind as to prepare her for burial, just now, and I decided to go for a walk—"

"An' here I'm sceerin' the b'jeesus outta ye!" Sean interjected.

"No, no. Just a bit jumpy, that is all. Not your fault."

He decided to change the subject, for both talking about and, more precisely, *seeing,* his dead wife had taken its toll on his nervous system. "How's your brother's ankle doing? I have been meaning to come over and check in on him. Things have just gotten a bit..." His voice trailed off.

Sean got to his feet and offered a hand to Dr. Arless, which he accepted. "Timmy's just fine, sir. Ye fixed'im up good, you did. Should be completely fit fer the harvest."

"Good. Glad to hear it."

Suddenly, something occurred to Dr. Arless. It was both appalling and exhilarating at how quickly his mind worked in this way. It would be a slap in the face disguised as a gesture of good will. Not to Sean; he neither liked nor disliked the young man. He merely tolerated him, the way he tolerated roast chicken when his palate was meant for fois gras. It would be a slap in the face of the good Vicar Pratt.

"Forgive me, Sean, I hope I am not being too forward when I ask this, but how is your family's financial predicament?"

"Ye know 'ow it is fer folk like me. Six of us t'feed an' only me an' Timmy able t'work. An' not much out there fer the likes of us, other than helpin' in the fields an' ditch diggin'."

A wet smile widened on Dr, Arless's face. "How would you like to make an easy guinea for one night's work?"

Sean's eyes widened. "I—I don't know what t'say. Thank ye, sir! Thank ye dearly. I ne'er held that much money in me hands all at once. That's awfully kinda ye, doctor, sir. That kinda money can put some good food on th'table for a long while, long while, indeed! Whatcha got in mind fer me?"

"Watching over my beloved for me."

5

The doctor returned home and, after some explaining as to why he was drenched in river water, retired to his room.

Thus dry and clothes replaced, he lay upon his bed, staring at the ceiling, hoping against hope that Gwen would stay out of his thoughts and, more importantly, out of his room.

Soon, though, a fitful slumber overtook him. He dreamt happily, at first, of travel, sun, drink, parties, and pretty ladies. Yet during a flirting dance with these unknown beauties, they would metamorphose into his wife. However, these weren't old recollections of the two happily dancing at some festivity long past. In each instance she would bend into him smiling and whisper seductively in his ear, "I'm still alive." And when she pulled back from the whisper, her pale smooth skin began to drop from her like melting tallow, exposing muscle and bone that dribbled blood onto his suit. The gentle touches of hands and waist transformed into boney, noose-tight clutches around his neck. She seemed hell-bent on taking him to the grave with her.

In only a short while, he awoke abruptly to a stealthy noise, a gentle ruffle and quick, dainty footsteps just outside his door.

"Olivia?" he called out rubbing his eyes. "Olivia, is that you? I am decent. Would you be a dear and come in and take these wet clothes to be laundered? I'm dreadfully sorry. I should have put them in the hallway earlier for you to take."

More discreet shuffling but no response.

Dr. Arless quickly arose from his bed with a quickly rising dread and went to the door, hesitating briefly before opening it just a sliver.

"Olivia?"

A wisp of white lace flashed quickly across his vision.

He quickly closed the door, leaning on it for support, his heart an odd, quick syncopation; with only a momentary glance, he but knew that what he had seen was the dress his wife was to be buried in.

No, that couldn't be it. It had to be yet another phantasm with which his entire day had been plagued.

He rubbed the remaining sleep from his eyes and listened intently for more ghostly din. All seemed quiet now outside the door. Still, he listened another long minute.

Nothing.

The doctor slowly opened the door just wide enough to reconnoiter the hallway just beyond. Less than a hand's width away from his peeping eye was one of the same — dead, cataract, veiled in white crepe — staring back at him. A foul stench permeated the miasma between them.

"I'm still alive!" it clacked through the crack in the door.

Dr. Arless slammed it shut and stuttered back to his bed. "Leave me alone! You're not alive. You're dead! I made sure of that! I couldn't have been wrong. I did it myself. You are dead, and this is just a figment of my distressed mind!"

The crystal glass door knob bit by bit twisted and unlatched with a quiet *click*.

A creak upon its hinges whispered, as the door slowly opened.

Climbing onto his bed, Dr. Arless shielded himself with his covers in a puerile attempt at protection from the ghoul beyond the door. "You are dead! Dead, I say. I had to do it. I had to! Leave me alone!"

"Had to do what, sir?" Olivia queried as she entered the room.

She saw his ashen face, muscles twisted and contorted in fear. She ran to him. "Sir, what's come over you?"

His speech was quick with fear. "You saw her, yes? Gwen. Just outside the door. In her burial gown. You saw her, didn't you?"

She gently unlatched the blanket from his grip and helped him down off the bed. "Sir, the missus is down stairs, in her room, waiting for the casket and the mourners for the service. I am sure she is not wandering the halls."

"So you didn't see her then?"

"No, sir."

With a blank stare, almost absentmindedly, he said, "Di—did you need me for something?"

"No, sir. I was just coming up to tell you the vicar's wife has finished dressing her. I wanted to know if there was anything I could do for you before I start getting ready. Everyone will be here at six and Mr. Timmons with the casket sometime before that."

She grabbed a small, red velvet stool from Mrs. Arless's vanity and sat it by the open window and opened up the drawn curtains. She gently led him to the chair. "Come, sir. Sit. What you're seeing are the ghosts of a troubled mind. You loved the missus. She is dead. It is proper to think she is still alive when she is not. The day is bright and warm and the breeze, most pleasant. Sitting here will clear the cobwebs from your mind, if you let it."

"So I shall. Yes, only ghosts of a troubled mind. Yes, I think I'll sit for a while."

Dr. Arless sat motionless, hands on his knees, staring blankly out into wheat fields and the church just beyond.

And Olivia left the room with new tears falling from her cheeks.

. . . .

The doctor was roused some time later by the clapping of horses' hooves along the cobbled way in front of his home. However, his eyes never strayed from the graveyard beyond the wheat field—Gwen's new permanent home; a residence in which she could not take up soon enough, as far as he was concerned. He had squeezed what little life she had left from her and ever since had been tormented by a putrid spirit who claimed she was still alive. Her body had not miraculously revived since he lifted the pillow from her head more than eight hours ago. She never stirred when they cleaned and powdered her flesh and dressed her for burial. Yet, he now wondered if indeed she was still amongst the living, in a deep, unconscious slumber from which she could wake at any moment and tell the tale of his black transgression.

The thought of being found out made his heart leap almost as much as seeing the decaying form of his wife. His constitution was not one that could bear the hardships of prison and his neck, too weak to hold a noose. The sole purpose of his foray into medicine was to attract someone of higher caliber than he otherwise might have warranted because of the lowly situation he had been born into. He was put into this world to be in comfort not to toil. To think that he might end up like those with whom he grew up appalled him beyond anything he could endure.

He had worked too hard, harder than most, to attain the standing he now had. Even though he had grown to love her in his own way, his wife was but a means to an end. An end he now possessed and would fight to keep.

It was these feelings that sparked within him the courage to do what needed done for the better aim of both of them. That is, at least, what he had told himself, as he wrenched the pillow around his sick wife's face.

Now, however, his weak constitution and love of life's better comforts haunted him as much as did his dead Gwen.

There were struggled footsteps on the front porch that fully broke him from this grim reverie, and he looked away from the church for the first time. This must be the special casket finally arriving. Shortly, they would be rearranging the sitting room and placing the body within in preparation for a hasty viewing before burial. He would stay in his room until the morbid display was ready.

. . . .

The doctor got dressed without looking at all in the full length mirror for fear of the possibility that the dead/not dead abomination would be staring back at him from beyond the glass.

He rang Olivia up so he would spend no time alone between his bedroom and the sitting room, which now housed the casketed body of his wife.

When he finally appeared at the top of the staircase, several sets of forlorn eyes stared unblinkingly, waiting his descent: There was Gwen's best friend, Ellie Todd, who accompanied the Arlesses on many of their trips to the continent; Sarah Terrill and her husband, Gwen's cousin and the only relative within a short enough distance to attend the hastened service; three close acquaintances from the church, Mary Aslip, Dorcas Pelham, and Maddie Ives; lastly, there was the vicar, his wife, and Mr. Timmons. In total there were eleven souls, including the widower, himself, and Olivia.

With the doctor thus descended and given consolations from all there, the vicar waved silence to the small crowd to begin his hastily prepared sermon.

The words to beckon off Gwen to the great Beyond were but muffled chatter in the doctor's ears. His attention was completely given over to the queer looking casket and its contents in the room to his left. In almost all respects, it looked like any other casket; it was a polished, dark mahogany trimmed in gold leaf and polished brass, with a padded lining of white silk stitched in intricate patterns. The bottom half of the lid was lowered and latched into place over Gwen's body, while the upper half was open for the mourners to get one last glimpse of the deceased.

There were but a few exceptions to this elegant *boite de la mort*: Dr. Arless noticed the exophytic, threaded one foot piece of polished brash in the middle of the opened lid, no doubt the fixture for the fresh air to be circulated from the land of the living above the burial site; and there was lastly a small, polished brass rod, at the top of which was an eyehole. This arose from the edge of the coffin near the dead woman's crossed arms. This must have been a fixture for the rope Mrs. Arless would use when she miraculously awoke from her near-death slumber and rang the bell aboveground to be loosed from her soiled prison.

Dr. Arless shuddered noticeably at its phantom ringing in his ear.

Heads nodded in unison around him as Vicar Pratt waxed eloquent on behalf of Dr. Arless's dead wife. The doctor only began to pay attention when the old Anglican priest began the descent on his eulogy.

He was completely pulled back to this grim reality when he felt himself being pulled and prodded, as a que was forming in the entranceway to pass by and view Gwen one last time. All seemed to yield at once for the doctor to lead the que, however he had seen more of his dead wife than he'd cared to share, so he insisted that he be the last to pass her casket.

Once each person passed, they quickly went outside to their carriage and waited for the procession to the grave site.

It was Dr. Arless's turn, in due course, and he quickly swept up Olivia by the arm. "Let's both see her together, as she meant the world to us both," he regarded with a slight quiver in his voice.

Olivia, knowing how troubled the doctor's mind had been earlier, had stayed behind precisely as a comfort for the doctor, as he viewed his wife one last time. She smiled meekly and tucked her hand under his arm.

With a deep breath by one and a sob by the other, they entered the room to say their goodbye.

With trepidation, Dr. Arless advanced to the casket, hesitating momentarily, almost turning to leave. Olivia, however, would not let him go. "Please, sir. Say your goodbye, or you'll live to regret it, and you'll never have this moment again."

With an ever sickening mind the doctor was already regretting this moment. Yet, without realizing it, he was now at the casket looking down on his wife. Her ginger hair had been washed and curled. Heavy makeup covered the pustules on her forehead and cheeks, and rouge had been lastly added to the crusty layers.

Besides this, however, she merely looked asleep, and that is what still troubled the doctor; she merely looked asleep—a deep, unconscious sleep, waiting for that climactic moment when, for reasons unknown, her brain and heart would become active once more, she would awaken, and her haunting would then take a physical turn.

After a quiet moment, Olivia kissed her gloved hand, placed it on Gwen Arless's heart, and sobbed into the background, leaving Dr. Arless there alone.

He looked back at her nervously, as his housemaid went back into the foyer with the men standing about waiting to take the coffin for its somber trip to the cemetery.

When he turned back to his wife, though he couldn't be certain in his state of mind, it seemed there was now an ever so slight smile on her face where once before there was not. The makeup had ridged into crusty wrinkles about the edges of her lips where before none had been.

The dead woman was mocking him.

His heart leapt into his throat, and he suddenly felt nauseous. As best he could, without casting undue anxiety, Dr. Arless turned and quickly left the room, the house, and hurried himself into his waiting carriage.

· · · ·

Sean Caudill was standing at the gravesite, uncomfortably kicking at the clumps of fresh earth piled to one side of the rectangular cavity when the carriages arrived. Nearby was a lantern and a stool. His tall frame cast an even longer shadow across the grass and graves from the low hanging sun to his back, beyond the wheat field.

The vicar was the first out of his carriage and cast a curious brow at Sean, as he approached the young man.

"Young Mr. Caudill, are you lost, boy? You've come at an inopportune moment. As you can see, we are preparing to bury Mrs. Arless. She died earlier today."

Sean bowed his head and took off his hat, twisting it nervously in his hands.

He was about to speak when Dr. Arless came up behind Vicar Pratt and explained. "Sorry, vicar. I guess I forgot to mention it earlier; I ran into Sean down at the river today and asked him if he would mind being the bell guard at Gwen's gravesite tonight. I hope I haven't stepped on anyone's toes."

"But I've already arranged for Mr. Severo to do it."

The doctor tried to hide a wry grin, quickly regained himself, and motioned the vicar to a private sidebar. "Apologies, vicar," the doctor lied, "but surely you can't object to giving the job to the one most needing of the generosity. You know as well as any the troubles of the Caudill family, and I promised a Guinea for the job."

"Yes, but..." He looked around to make sure no one could hear them and whispered, "The *troubles*, as you say, they bring on themselves with more drink and less food with what little money they *do* make."

He hesitated a moment then whispered ever softer, "You do know they are *Papists* don't you?"

The doctor put on a façade of irritation. "Where they attend church had no bearing in my decision," he said in a melodramatically impenitent tone, "and it shouldn't enter into yours, as well."

The old man sighed, scratched his balding head, and his face reddened, as well, if only for a different reason. "Yes, yes. Your remonstration is deserved and correct. He would be precisely the kind of person to whom your wife would have steered her charity. Yet, Mr. Severo… What should I tell him?"

Dr. Arless did not try to hide his smile when he said, "That, vicar, will be your problem to rectify." And with that, the doctor broke ranks with the vicar and sauntered over to his young sentry.

When Sean gave him a querying look, Dr. Arless assured him, "Everything is fine. The vicar didn't know I had already made arrangements with you and had employed the services of Mr. Severo to guard the gravesite."

The young man scratched at his surly golden locks as he asked, "Sir, you've yet t'tell me—what 'zactly am I guarding th'grave from?"

"From the unlikely prospect of my wife coming back to life and ringing the bell they will be attaching shortly to her dead hand. If that happens, you will be charged with digging her up."

Sean's face became noticeably pale, giving more distinction to his freckle-pocked face. "I don't mind sharin' wi' Mr. Severo, if that'll help. He seems a nice man, he does, an' looks kindly at me when we pass in th'village. Though he oft looks like he got the morbs," he quickly added.

The doctor patted him on the shoulder. "No, no, that won't be necessary. I'm paying for your services, and you should get the entire amount." He fished from the pocket of his suit a gold coin. He made sure no one was looking when he gave it to Sean. "One Guinea, as promised."

"This is most generous, sir." The young man's voice cracked. His eyes widened and teared when he felt the shiny piece in his hands, turning it over in admiration. "Can't thank ye' nuff, sir, for this, truly."

When he looked back up, he only saw that back of the doctor, who was now ten feet away, headed back to the others.

From over his shoulder Dr. Arless retorted, "Just stay back behind a tree till the service is over."

6

The service and burial had been the most grueling two and a half hours he had endured in quite a long while. It seemed to be a fitting cap on the head of a Jekyll and Hyde day. It had been both exhilarating and horrifying—the exhilaration of freedom from an ever-growing burden, and the horror of the haunting of a dead wife who may not be dead.

Now back in his bedroom, Dr. Arless shed his suitcoat, not bothering to pick it up from the floor, unbuttoned his collar, and charged straight to a small mahogany bar next to his dresser. He poured himself a whisky, which burned but didn't cleans his palate of the char of the past twelve hours.

He had found within himself a darkness that had simmered just below the surface of his soul, simmered and seethed for years. In the months leading up to this morning, that simmer turned to a bubble, then a boil, until that pot frothed over with fully cooked indignation. This morning he had feasted on it. Now, he was full.

Exhausted, the doctor finally and reluctantly changed into his night clothes, although it was only just before 9:00, and donned his silk housecoat.

He then looked over his spirits one more time until he found a suitable companion.

Dr. Arless finally exchanged the dainty stool at the window for a more comfortable high back from his side of the room, lit the candles on his nightstand, and resolved to watch the waning day bleed itself out with a full snifter of cognac.

Rolling the honey colored liquid around softly in its glass, Dr. Arless settled in and regarded the scene outside his bedroom window. The horizon was burnt by the melting sun, and was no longer blemished with clouds. The night would be clear and cool.

Tiny, multiform gravestones in the distance, like grey mold amongst the gold and green, caught his eye, and he wondered how his charge was doing amongst the dead and possibly dead.

At that thought, he took his first long swill of alcohol, not bothering to savor the flavor or aroma of the cognac, only to hasten its last desired trait—inebriation. Without a single morsel of food yet eaten, that state for which he now worked so diligently came surprisingly quick.

. . . .

The vicar slalomed between gravestones, lantern held high, racing as quickly as his old bones would allow.

Sean Caudill could be heard cursing somewhere in the shadows above the clinking clamor of the grave bell.

At last, the old man of God stumbled upon the grave. And there he eyed a tipped stool, an upturned flask still spilling its contents into the fresh dirt, and Sean Caudill tangled in the roping of the grave bell, lantern by his side. With each yank and pull, as he tried to undo himself, the bell would sound its alarm.

"Mr. Caudill, do you know what you've just done?" the vicar lamented.

"S-sorry, vicar, sir. I was—I was just goin' t'relieve meself, an'…"

"You've been taking the drink, boy! You're arse over elbow there!"

"Only t'keep meself warm, nothin' more, I swear."

"I knew I should have insisted on Mr. Severo," he grunted, as he began to undo the web of rope Sean Caudill had woven around his leg.

"I'm not blatted. I'd not disrespect th'good Arless name, I swear by it. I tripped meself up on a bloody clump a dirt."

"For your sake, young man, I hope the ringing from this blasted bell hasn't reached the ears of our neighbors. I can only imagine what hearing it would do to Mr. Arless' nerves. Olivia has intimated that he's not been taking this as well as he seems."

There was a sudden scream in the distance that carried on the cooling midnight breeze.

The vicar sighed. "That would more than likely be Olivia now. If she has heard the bell, then Mr. Arless, no doubt, has as well."

He finally completely untied the young man from his bonds. "You, my boy, get back on that stool and do not stray from it till I return," he snorted irritably. "When I return, there had better be no alcohol left in that flask — and I do not mean its disappearance by drink."

Sean nodded with sheepish hesitation without looking directly at the vicar and returned his stool upright.

A second, more horrific, scream made both men jump.

The vicar's features set grimly in the harsh lamplight. "I guess I'll have to walk down and tell them that the ringing was you. I'm not sure what I'll find when I get there; but they must be told that Mrs. Arless definitely *is not* alive."

. . . .

A noise woke Dr. Arless from an alcohol induced slumber. The sun had long set, and stars now glittered the night sky beyond the window. A cool evening current crawled into the room, and their chilly fingers helped caress the doctor back to consciousness.

Upon wiping the cobwebs away, he realized the cognac snifter was no longer in his hand. He leaned over the arm of the chair only to see it broken on the hardwood floor near his feet with its contents in small, sticky pools.

Even before he could blaspheme the ruination of good crystal and even better spirits, Dr. Arless heard the din that revived him from his alcoholic coma.

He struggled at first to ascertain what the noise was and from whence it came. His eyes quickly darted around the room, fearing that another wifely specter had come to torment him.

The only ghosts were the souls of the candlelight dancing upon the walls.

When he heard the faint, haphazard ringing a third time, the doctor's heart leapt painfully into his throat, making him momentarily gag in horror.

He staggered over himself and thrust his torso out the open window, squinting in the direction of the graveyard. The lantern light zigged in one direction then zagged in another, all the while the grave bell tinkled wildly and sporadically, seconds of nothing, then frantic ringing and ringing, then nothing again.

Poor Sean Caudill was probably beside himself in fear, not knowing what was happening and unsure what to do.

Who would have thought that this would actually happen? In the back of everyone's mind, this guard post was but a formality of futility.

But there was no mistaking the sound; Gwen Arless was still alive, and his devilish deed would be found out by all.

Suddenly, the bedroom door exploded open. It crashed back against, then bounced off of, the side wall. In ran Gwen Arless, no longer covered in earth and eaten by death. She looked as healthy as she had so long ago before the disease began to eat her alive.

Dr. Arless's head spun like a top from his bedroom door back out to the graveyard where he was still hearing the clanging of the grave bell. How could she be in the earth, yet here at the same time?

He regarded her once again, chest heaving, heart pounding, head spinning, terror building.

The once dead now alive again Gwen Arless screamed in a shrill voice, "I'm still Alive, I'm still Alive, I'm still alive, she's still alive!"

Unexpectedly, Dr. Arless's hand lost its footing on the window sill. With more of his upper body outside than inside, he had no way to right that sinking ship and fell from the window.

In that tumble, as he peered through his upended legs, and before the view of the bedroom was briefly replaced by the glinting night sky, Dr. Arless caught one last glimpse of the woman in his room. It seemed Gwen Arless had once again been replaced by another; his last view was of Olivia with a look of horror upon her face.

He heard a brief scream, replaced by a wet *crack,* then all went black.

Jack

Jack. Jack, I like that nickname. Only my closest acquaintances call me Jack, and the post is proof that my inner circle is ever widening.

Jack. It has certain qualities that appeal to me. It is a one-syllable name, and no one should waste lung capacity on any name longer than that. It is a hard, uncompromising name. There is nothing in the sound of it that denotes indecisiveness.

Jack. I kill like my nickname—quick and decisive.

Tonight is the night. The moon knows. It is hiding behind a wet blanket of clouds the color and consistency of drab wool. Oh, occasionally, it peeks out momentarily, but once it sees my distinct silhouette upon the dank cobblestones of Whitechapel, it whips up those dingy covers over its head, once more.

Gaslights barely cut through the vaporous London filth, leaving most anything beyond ten feet of their glowing halo in undulating darkness. That darkness and I are inextricably linked. It envelopes me like the welcoming embrace of a friend and ushers me along the back alleys, unseen, where I prefer to do my business; where the whores and prostitutes dole out their vile bodies for nothing more than a pittance.

Tonight, another lucky one will confer her body to me, but it will be for my pleasure, not hers. The thought of my pleasure makes me smile, but my friend the darkness sweeps it into the shadows under my rimmed felt hat, as I pass under a lamp post and turned left onto Duke Street.

A little farther along, and I will turn down Church Passage towards Mitre Square; I have business there.

I feel inside my caped coat and find the polished steel that I will use in my endeavor. It is long, sharp, and slightly slick from the blood of my first catch. I wiped it is haste on the trollop's dress, but it did not come completely clean. I can feel its cold comfort through my leather gloves. It transfers to my touch a longing that entices me to quicken my pace—just a little.

My hands also trace along the bulge of my belly through the thick lining of my coat. Tucked into the front of my shirt is a linen bag from the hospital. My employer never misses them. They have more than they can ever account for. Within that bag is my post mortem attire; I loathe being in soiled clothing. This bag sits in my front in such a way as to make me look paunchy, like so many Englishmen. In reality, I am lean, so my torso amalgamates with the linen bag quite well. Any abnormalities from concealing this under my shirt is further hidden under my full-length coat.

I also feel—but do not rattle—my full change purse. It is the bait that will be cast into the slimy sea of prostitutes.

The fish are hungry. They are always hungry.

As am I, yet my hunger doesn't subside with a full belly but with bloody hands.

As I begin to turn into Church Passage, the onset of my affliction is lightning-quick. I have to stop. Everything is silent when my footfalls cease. This area between the street lamps and passage is coffin dark but not reassuring to my sense of seclusion.

I look around the stone and glass cemetery around me for an even darker refuge. None is darker than where I am about to proceed so I quickly stagger ahead.

My head is pounding as though being pummeled under the hoof of a draught horse, and my equilibrium leaves me like an exhaled breath.

I finally take asylum in that narrow walkway. Its darkness is soothing and complete, but its length and narrowness fosters within me a feeling of staring down the mouth of a well that stretches to the very bowels of the earth. My dizziness lies to me, telling me that lifting my feet would be tantamount to lunging headlong down that forever-falling fount.

After a few labored steps into that tarry gloom, so as not to be seen by any improbable passers-by, I clutch and pull myself to the cold, dank wall just in case that fiction of falling transforms into fact.

I squeeze my face, as if the pressure I apply will force the vileness within me out through my ears. This vileness is Syphilis. My experience tells me it is in its final stages. In this tertiary stage, Syphilis will manifest itself by causing severe pain and vertigo, hallucinations, and dementia, to name but a few.

Some of these symptoms affect me, but it is not dementia that inclines me to slice and eviscerate prostitutes; one of those bottom feeders infected me so many years ago. I was young and adventuresome, a free spirit who was willing to try anything with anyone in the pursuit of pleasure. I was ruled more by my groin than my brain or my heart. It was folly, I now know, but the young always seem to think their humanity is covered in a suit of armor. I was different in many respects, but in that respect I was a rank-and-file youth who thought they could get away with eating the poisonous mushroom and come out unscathed.

Now, that poison was eating my brain. I am not so far gone that I think I can rid the world of all its overgrowth of weeds, but I at least can give it a trim around the edges.

Besides, I have found out by the purest of happenstance that I also like doing it. There is a certain feeling of contentment that wells within me after my business is done, not unlike, no doubt, that which Michelangelo felt after completing one of his frescos. Like him, I am the master of my medium.

I repress a tormented scream that has boiled up to my lungs from the pot of pain in my belly. If it advances any further, I will give myself away. I squeeze my face harder to keep that torment within me, lest it escape with the force of a North Sea gale.

I have a small bottle of laudanum to ease the pain, but I loathe drinking it before doing my business. It numbs my senses and lessens the enjoyment I would otherwise have playing with a wench's internal organs. I will use it, if need be, but I decide to wait and see if the ordeal passes. Sometimes its onset and demise can be a matter of only minutes; occasionally, the agony can last hours.

Just when I think the pain is at its most unbearable and reach for the small bottle in my pocket, the pain relinquishes its iron grasp on me. It leaves me exhausted. I resist the urge to retch because I am strong.

Syphilis may eventually win the war, but I have won every battle since taking up the fight.

I inhale deeply to give much needed air to my struggling lungs. This renews me, and I need as much strength as can be mustered this night. Much energy was used just a short while ago with my first go of the night but not as much as I would have liked; someone in a dogcart was boorish enough to interrupt my opus.

This grip of pain, having thus unhanded me, was not entirely unexpected. Its intensity, however, though short in duration, was one of greater magnitude than any previous. It takes several more deep inhalations to restore my vigor.

Suddenly, footsteps near the far end of the passage sober me fully. She is coming from the direction on Mitre Square but has not yet reached the entrance to Church Passage. How convenient it is that my prey comes to me, this time.

The outline to most at this distance would be indiscernible, but the darkness is my friend. It whispers in my ear in the form of quick, delicate steps that the shadow is female.

As if ushering her to her demise, fingers of fog, vaguely phosphorescent from a far-off gas light, wrap themselves around her, as she starts down the passage.

There is only one kind of fish in the sea at this hour. It is time to cast another lure.

As our paths narrow, my steps are longer and faster and quieter. She may not even know of my presence as yet.

We are nearer to Mitre Square than Duke Street, from which I had just turned.

I can sense apprehension in the woman — just a little. She now sees my blackened outline ahead of her. Her steps slacken then resume their original pace, scraping a heel of her shoe on the walkway, almost stumbling. Considering the deeds I've done over the last few weeks, I suppose I should not blame her. She has reason to be fearful; fate has put her in the path of Jack the Ripper.

See, even Destiny is unwilling to protect those such as this contemptable creature, who will give away her most precious asset for the smallest morsel or pittance of coin, not even being civilized enough to keep herself clean for those to whom she sells.

I will now free her of that burden.

She is within striking distance.

I rattle my change purse loud enough for her to realize my intentions.

She slows down and nods. "Evenin', sir."

I tip my hat and disguise my voice, though I probably have no good reason to do so to catch a fish such as this. "Will you?" I ask.

She stood a moment, perfectly still, as though ascertaining my qualities through the inky night between us.

I can smell the trepidation in the space between us.

She begins to walk past without reply, but I grab her by the arm.

Once again, I rattle my change purse. "Twice what you usually ask, if you will. If you will, please." I think it beneath me to plead, but I am in character. A paunchy, old Englishman like myself would no doubt have to plead, even if a little, to get a woman to open up for me.

Her shadowed head turns, briefly, inspecting the coal-black walkway behind us. She turns her head back to me, up the passageway, then back to me once more. I can tell by the slight widening of her shadowed cheeks that a smile has puckered her face in acquiescence. It's too bad that her last smile would be wasted on me.

She begins lifting her dress, as she says in a whisky-hardened voice, "Twice it is, then, and you won't regret what you pay for, if I do say so myself, sir."

This is when I am at my best. I am an expert at this grizzly business. I know precisely when to strike and how. I am ambidextrous in this tenebrous murk and know my way around a body by a sense that few others possess. It is this awareness that strengthens my bravado to do something no other would dare try nearly sightless and with stepped up patrols in every quarter of Whitechapel.

My hands are surprisingly lightning-quick and tourniquet-tight, and they strike at the woman's neck while her hands are fumbling around the dirty cloth of her dress.

I force her back towards Mitre Square then up against the gritty wall, as my hands clench off the blood supply to her brain and squeeze shut her windpipe, refusing her the ability to scream.

She struggles violently, as they all do, but she is quickly using up what little air she has left in her lungs. She only manages to push against my face. She swings her hands wildly only to land fruitless blows to my shoulder.

The only sounds our intimate embrace surrender are a few shuffles of feet against cobblestone and the faint wheeze of a clenched-off windpipe.

There always arises in me at these times a revulsion-induced strength that I would otherwise not possess. My hands compress, like the coils of a constrictor, around her neck, and I almost believe that I have the capacity to pop her head completely off her shoulders.

She tries with what little energy she retains for one last attempt to free herself from my grip, but my forearms are plastered against her shoulders, my legs are firmly lodged between hers, pressing outward to keep her off balance. All she can do is wiggle like a hooked cod pulled up from the abyss on a fishing line.

A hand briefly breaks free, however instead of striking at me, she tries to maneuver her hand to her body. She is surprisingly quick, as she reaches for something under her shawl; I might have misjudged just how close to death she was. Some succumb quickly to my grip. Others aren't so ready to give up the ghost. This one's a fighter, and that, itself, heightens my arousal for blood.

I feel tempered steel brush up against my forearm. Well, well! She carries protection. Since my implement is sullied, I will use hers when the time comes.

Though she manages to retrieve the knife, I do not give her enough use of her arm to use it with any effect. She manages to stick its point in my coat sleeve, cutting the outer shell, but it is not with enough force to rend all the layers and get at my skin.

I momentarily free my left hand from its death grip and catch her armed hand as its blade tried to find traction on flesh. I smash her knuckles against the wall. After two such blows, she whimpers painfully, loses the grip on the blade, and it falls in a metallic *clank* upon the damp macadam.

I then quickly resume my constriction.

I give her credit. That was an admirable attempt. But even with one interrupted session and an unbearable attack of pain, I, even in a weakened state, am more than she can handle.

Her muscles slacken underneath my grip. The hiss of her cut-off screams lessons.

I begin to move her along the wall, hand-to-hand and hand-to-throat in a death-waltz. I like to dance; it helps to drain completely that little bit of life they scratch and claw to keep.

Ah, four minutes until she gives up the ghost. More than I would have preferred but not bad, all things considered.

Through an alchemic process heretofore unknown, she transfers her life force into me; her limp body empowers my now weakened and aching muscles. This has been a grueling night, even for the likes of me, but her death makes me strong again.

As I lay her down, I smell the pestilent fog. The dead give off a scent. This scent is like a delicate perfume to my nostrils, invigorating me to gut my catch.

I retrace our dance from its end to where we first embraced. I find her dropped knife in a shallow puddle of rainwater at the base of the passage wall and quickly return to my pile of cloth and flesh and set about my work.

I am happy at my task, content even, resisting the urge to hum a tune, as I feel the slickness between my gloved fingers in the dark.

Then it strikes again. The pain sears me like a hot iron poked through my eyes, into my brain. I bite down hard on and through my blood-soaked glove to repress a scream of pain. I taste globs of wet copper, and I am unsure how much of it is hers and how much may be mine, as my teeth break the skin.

Recently, I have noticed the quickening pace of these attacks. They are becoming more pronounced, more unbearable. When the insufferable ones sink their claws into my head, I have been lucky enough to find temporary refuge in empty rooms, back alleys, and wooded parks until they subside.

I know the future holds no sway in my providence for keeping the affliction to myself. The only one who knows at present is my friend the night. That is how it shall remain until such a time arrives when I can no longer keep control of my senses. I will not spend the rest of my days locked in an asylum room, staring out through the London fog at the pestilence peddling their wares on the street below. I will take my own life when the time comes. It could be said that I will die in childbirth. That newborn's brain will hold an insight for hatred in all its glorious colors, its limbs shall be formed for murder, its heart will pump only apathy, its eyes shall be blind to goodness, its ears deaf to mercy, its tongue will taste only blood and it will suckle on indignation. It will understand only self-preservation. The only love it will give and get in kind is love of death. History will look back on me and say that I gave birth to the modern age.

Instead of repressing that all-encompassing pain, I turn it into an all-consuming anger that jolts my hands like lightning strikes. These bolts of hatred are concentrated around the woman's face. I stab, I cut, I gouge, I slice, until I am completely drained.

The night-cloaked dagger drips the aftermath, as I clutch my head once more and drop to my knees.

Deciding that prudence at this point is best if I am to carry on my endeavors beyond this night, I pull the laudanum from my pocket. It won't take effect right away, but I will begin to feel its numbing effects when I put a block between me and my work.

I open the vial and drink.

I also pull from my coat a small leather satchel. I put a few trinkets from my handiwork inside for later use, pull the drawstring, and my onyx companion whisks me off into the damp and dingy night, as unseen as that cowering moon.

I am not done playing. There are a few things yet needing prepared before I call it an evening.

Two blocks away, already feeling the deadening effects of the drug, I find a small alcove hidden in the shadows that services a butcher shop. It is in this comforting darkness where I change into my post-mortem attire. I put my bloody gloves, ripped coat, trousers and shirt, even my felt hat, into the linen bag.

I then walk several more blocks to London Bridge. There, before I walk across, I pick up a heavy stone from the walkway and place it into the linen bag. This, I toss into the Thames' muddy water when I am at the bridge's midway point before heading off to my next playground.

After catching my limit fishing for prostitutes, I turn my endeavors to playing with the bobbies. I scribble some graffiti about Jews on a wall and drop a clue that will drive them mad. Then, it will be time to retire for the evening.

. . . . .

It's nearly three in the morning when I finally arrive back home. I try to be as quiet as possible when entering the house, even leaving the hansom a block from home to keep the *clap* of hoof-upon-cobblestone from waking the questioning eyes of neighbors.

Instead of going directly to bed, I spend time in the bathroom. Candlelight flickers my distorted shadow across the wall, as I pour then splash water on my face and stare at the reflection in the mirror. This is the first time the reflection looks weary.

My hands shake, my ears ring like the insides of a tolling bell.

My time at play in this filthy world is nearing its inevitable end.

From another room I hear a tired voice call out, "Jack? That you, dear?"

I say nothing. I just stare at the wilting face before me; at one time it was such a beautiful face. Now, it is but a shell of what it used to be.

There is a knock at the door, then a sleepy-eyed face peaks in. "Jack?"

I still only stare back at myself, unblinking at what Syphilis has done to me. Eyes once the color of a clear summer sky are now dull and gray. My cheeks have sunken and my chin protrudes. The once delicate features of a woman are now being eaten away. This transformation has seemingly happened within the time span of a single evening.

"Jacqueline, you alright?" he implores with patient concern.

I unfasten and let down my long, blond hair then run my fingers through their thinning strands. "Sorry, love," I sigh. "It's been a long night."

He extends a sleepy smile. "Got your cable about staying late tonight at the hospital, but didn't think you would've been this long."

"Nor I, dearest," I reply. "Sometimes the sick have their own schedule. Tonight they conspired against me at every turn."

"You know I worry about you at these hours."

"I know."

"This bloody Jack the Ripper nonsense and all that."

"Jack kills prostitutes," I clarify.

"Sometimes it might be hard to tell the difference in the dark."

"Jack knows."

"You talk as though you know the man."

"I know the type. I see a lot working where I do."

"I still worry."

"I know you do."

He yawns and scratches his head. "You coming to bed soon, then?"

"I'll be right in, love."

He blows me a kiss and says, "I'll warm up your side of the bed for you," then slowly closes the door.

James is such a wonderful man. So innocent and ignorant. He loves me so unconditionally. It's truly unfortunate that he will have to die, too. He is a flower among the weeds, an Angel fish among the bottom dwellers. So in my benevolence, I will spare him the blade; I have passed on my affliction to him.

They say that sharing with your partner that which is most intimate is a sign of true love. And Jack does so love death.

The Thing in the Shadows

1

The bear of a man looked around the smoke-filled den, holding a handkerchief over his nose. It was the first time—and hopefully the last—he had ever been inside this kind of establishment. Men lay back languidly on velvet couches, long pipes loosely grasped, or sprawled out on Persian carpets, many curled up in little balls in the darkened and hazy corners. Beaded entranceways that led to other rooms clapped lightly to an unseen disturbance at the far end, only barely discernable in the noxious fog of the place.

Somewhere among this slapdash amalgam of barely conscious bodies was Alastair Wiggins.

The man removed the cloth and yelled out in a voice as thick as his girth, "Alastair? Alastair, you in here?"

No one replied.

Then he remembered the man's father saying that Alastair now went by his middle name, so he tried that, as well. "Wendell, then? Is Wendell Wiggins here?"

Although he wasn't sure the movement was voluntary, a limp figure splayed face down on a rug made what appeared to be an attempt at raising his arm.

The big man took that as a yes, went to the smoke-shrouded figure, grabbed him up by his shirt, and whisked him back out the front door.

Outside, the air was crisp. The sun was angled acutely in the cloudless sky, which made the abductor drop his handkerchief and shield his eyes, as he clomped along the wooden walkway until he found what he was looking for. Adjacent to the front entrance was a water trough, into which the behemoth dropped the semi-conscious man.

A moment under the water and the man suddenly sprang back to life, flailing his arms wildly, grasping at the sides, coughing up horse-slobbered water. "Wha—what the hell? S-sir, how da-dare you. What is the meaning of this?"

He drew a fist but when he saw the size of the man it was meant for, he thought it better to use that hand to instead push the wet mop of hair from his eyes.

When his dizzy eyes finally whittled the three gentlemen in front of him down to one, he saw a smirk on the man's face.

"Son of a bitch. What'd you do that for, Arnold?" Wendell lamented, as he wobbly extracted himself from the trough.

"Probably the first bath you've had in a month," the big man replied.

As he steadied himself, trying to shake off the rest of the opium haze, Wendell said, "It is no one's concern how often I bathe. Who, exactly, would it be that I'd have to worry about offending?"

"Anyone within ten feet of you."

Reaching out a big hand to help steady him, Arnold then said, "That stuff'll kill you, you know."

"Again, it is no one's concern what I do to facilitate my death. It's my own, after all. Why not do it up the way you want? Up till just now, I didn't think anyone cared, anyway, least of all Father. What's he got you coming after me for now? He insisted I stay out of his life. I thought I'd done a pretty good job of that, these last four years."

The smile quickly disappeared from Arnold's cinder block of a face. "Everyone knows things between you and your father haven't always been good. I'd say there's been fault on both sides in your feud, but that ain't why I'm here."

Squeezing water from his shirt Wendell replied, "Spit it out, man. What does dear old dad want from me after so long a time?"

"Mr. Wiggins is dying. He's been down in Hamot Hospital a week now. He's slipping away, and he's asking for you."

Although they had their differences, Wendell didn't hate his father. Deep down one might say he fostered something akin to affection for the man, despite their troubled past. He only wished his father had felt the same way. He'd made his peace with that long ago—at the end of an opium pipe.

However, the thought of his father now dying sobered him fully.

"Take me to him," Wendell said somberly.

· · · · ·

The dog cart ride down to the hospital from the upper reaches of Parade Street was awkward and silent. Wendell remembered that his father's trusting servant wasn't the most adept at conversation as it was, but the particular kind of silence Arnold exhibited was unnerving, especially since the two hadn't seen each other in nearly four years; there was much to talk about. Wendell made several attempts at extracting helpful information as he dried himself off with some rags fetched from the back of the dog cart, but Arnold would only say the elder Mr. Wiggins was ill, dying and only asked to see Wendell as death neared. No allusion to what malady had overtaken the man, how long he'd been ill, or why he wanted to see his son before he died.

The only honest attempt at conversation was when Arnold had asked, "Why do you go by your middle name now?"

Wendell replied, "I figured it would help mask my relation to Father if I ever ran afoul of the law — not that I had planned to, mind you. But I know his standing in the community is not something to be trifled with."

"Wouldn't changing your last name've done a better job of that?" Arnold offered.

Wendell had only grinned and said, "But I rather like my last name."

Now, hands clasped nervously behind his back, Wendell stared out a window in the large, well-adorned hallway of the home-now-hospital. The bay, Presque Isle, and the lake lay just beyond at the bottom of the small hill on which the hospital sat. On the horizon, Lake Erie's blue water reflected the mid October sky. Only the schooners and steamers rippling the waters helped discern where lake started and sky ended.

Arnold sat contemplatively in a chair that seemed to be perpetually on the verge of being crushed under the weight of the man. His fixed stair would only wander from the door of Mr. Wiggins' room if Wendell happened to move from his sentry at the window.

Finally, after twenty minutes of waiting, a nurse exited the sick man's room.

"He's up now. I've arranged the room for him, and he's ready to see you."

"Thank you," answered Wendell.

"One thing, though, sir," the nurse went on in a solemn tone that matched to perfection her dark, close-set eyes and thin lips. "Do not, under any circumstances, close the curtains or blow out any of the candles."

Wendell cast a curious glance at Arnold, to which the man only nodded slightly his assent.

As he regarded the nurse again, she reiterated, "I cannot let you in unless you agree to leave the room as it is unless instructed otherwise by Mr. Wiggins himself. His orders, Mr. Wendell."

Curiosity rippled his brow but Wendell agreed, and the nurse moved aside to let him through.

At the threshold, Wendell turned to Arnold. "Aren't you coming in, too?"

Arnold, with a curiously fearful look in his eye, only shook his head no and stayed put on the tortured chair.

"Suit yourself."

Wendell went inside, closing the door behind him.

If the nurse hadn't already alluded to what was inside, the contents of the room would have done nothing if not pique his curiosity. To his immediate right were two large windows overlooking the bay and the lake. The curtains had been pushed completely aside, letting in the harsh autumn sun. A bed straddled the space between the windows and the sick Mr. Wiggins lay upon it, clutching his blankets.

But that wasn't the most curious thing about the room. In every corner and placed at intervals were a multitude of burning candles — twenty, at least — and three lit lanterns, all giving the appearance he was in the lantern room of a lighthouse staring into its Fresnel lens instead of the room of a dying man.

The unforgiving light made the opium cobwebs still hanging in Wendell's head stir in painful throbs.

A labored, phlegmy laugh brought him back to his father. "You look like hell," the sick man growled through wheezing breaths.

It was only then that Wendell realized how sloppy he looked and uncomfortable he felt in his still damp clothes.

"You can thank Arnold for my appearance."

"Whatever it was he did, I'm s-sure it was necessary. Come." He motioned to a chair next to the bed. "Sit."

Wendell did as requested. He knew from experience that any questions he might have would only be answered when his father was good and ready, so, as was protocol with the old horse shoe manufacturer, he took his seat next to the man and waited.

Although he could only be examined from the chest up, Wendell observed the hollow, bloodshot eyes, protruding cheeks, and ashen face — the countenance of one not long for this world.

After an awkward silence, the elder Wiggins finally spoke. "You're probably w-wondering why I called f-for you," he labored.

"I was hoping it was because you wanted to reconcile with your only son before you died," Wendell replied drily.

"In a m-manner of speaking, yes. There is something I need to t-tell you before I go."

"What, exactly, has you so ill?" he asked, knowing he had just broken protocol by doing so.

"What is k-killing me has no bearing on the outcome, now does it? Death is death no matter how you arrive at it. It is what's g-going to happen after I die."

"And what would that be?"

The sick man shuffled under his covers uneasily, clutching their edges as though they were the only thread that kept him tied to the mortal realm. He then stuttered out an unintelligible word that was cut off by a phlegmy cough. His eyes fearfully raced around the brightly lit room, as he regrouped his thoughts. Then he said in a forced whisper, "A-a demon, a *something*—I call it a demon, I don't know what else it could be—has tormented me f-for years. It's the damned reason why I'm in this bed. It'll have me soon enough, it's done with me. But not with us."

"Us? A what? What on earth are you talking about?"

"When I am gone it will come after you—come with one purpose and one only. It will come for your soul and try to get others. I-I gave it your soul. I gave you to it. I'm so sorry, son. I had to. I just couldn't s-stand the torment any longer."

Wendell gave his father an incredulous stare but said nothing.

"Oh, don't look at me like I'm a f-fool," the elder Wiggins rejoined.

"Just what kind of response were you expecting?" Wendell bit back. "I've not seen nor heard from you in nearly four years, I find you in a hospital bed, dying, and the first statement from your mouth is that I'm to be overtaken by some—some *demon*? And you—you *gave* it my soul? What the hell does that even mean?" Wendell threw up his hands in exasperation. "I'm speechless. I don't know what to say. Father, I know you think little of me, but at least do me the courtesy of an honest response."

"Oh, so you think I'm lying, d-do you?"

"What would you have me believe? That ghosts and ghouls are coming for my soul? How? For what purpose? You were never a believer in the hereafter, at least not that I am aware of, and *I* certainly am not. That is something that should have been instilled in me as a pup, not on your deathbed, for me to give it any credence."

"I see," the old man went on, "that I will have to c-convince you of it. No mind, I've already made ready with proof."

"Father, is this really necessary? I—"

"It is!" he cut in. "You don't understand. I'm doing this f-for you. So you can do something about it. It's too late for me. Maybe not for you."

Wendell rutted his brow and pushed back his still-damp, frenetic locks with a long sigh. "I don't understand Father."

The elder Wiggins, with much effort, extracted his hands from under the covers and pointed a trembling finger at two candles in the farthest corner of the room on the other side of a large wardrobe. "Those candles over there, the ones on the right, not the left, beyond that—yes, p-pick them up and take one step back from the corner."

Wendell did as asked and picked up the candles, one in each hand, and took one step back. "Now what?"

Mr. Wiggins took a labored breath and said in a broken voice, "N-now blow them out."

Not sure where these strange requests were going but settling easily back into the role of child-who-ever-wanted-to-please-his-father, Wendell blew out each of the candles.

"Now wha—"

Suddenly, within the shadows in the corner left by the snuffed candles, there arose movement that startled the young Wiggins. He glanced briefly back at his father, who had pulled the covers back over himself, cowering like a frightened mouse, which unnerved Wendell; he'd never seen his father recoil at anything.

When he looked back, the movement, initially only of different shades crisscrossing one another, had begun to take a definite form. It swirled about like oily snakes in an orgiastic, slithering ball.

The mass then became bigger, darker. Darker than the shadows in which it occupied.

Suddenly, two yellow eyes blinked open on the slithering mass.

He froze in terror, and his heart threatened to burst through his ribcage.

"Quickly, relight the c-candles!" Mr. Wiggins exclaimed between struggled breaths.

Wendell only stood, feet cemented to the floor, eyes as wide as two full moons, as the sour eyes within the mass fixed their unblinking glower upon him. His stomach, empty of food for two days, threatened to push its caustic fluid into his throat.

A black appendage slowly unraveled itself from the rest of the mass and reached out at Wendell with mottled, talon-like claws.

"Wendell!" his father exclaimed, then broke into a coughing fit.

The interjection broke the young man free from the initial shock. Although he was loath to turn his back on the freakish display in front of him, he did so, ran to the opposite corner, and quickly relit the candles from the lit ones there.

The candles shook violently as Wendell turned back around. He almost dropped them but quickly recovered himself before the fear of burning the hospital down became a reality.

As the light from the candles touched the slick, onyx mass, it mysteriously disappeared as quickly as it manifested.

He blinked twice in bewilderment, as he searched the corner for the thing that was only a moment ago manifest in the shadows there. "Wha...what in the hell was that?" he whispered, as if fear of saying it too loud would somehow summon it back. He slowly put down the candles and retreated back to his bedridden father, hands still quivering.

With much trouble catching his breath, the elder Wiggins replied, "That is nothing, my son, compared to what h-happens when there is no light to keep it at bay. That, that *thing* has been plaguing me since you were but a…but a boy. When I close my eyes in sleep or when t-the light goes…the light goes away."

Suddenly, as the elder Wiggins spoke, his color unexpectedly flushed from his face, and his breathing became noticeably more labored. He seemed on the verge of saying something else when his chest heaved twice, and he clutched himself, as a painful cry caught in his throat.

Wendell threw off the covers and pulled the man to him.

"Father?" Wendell pleaded. "Father!"

The elder Wiggins convulsed, two quick spasms, as he tried to focus on his son. His eyes passed from agony to fear to anger to almost, Wendell thought, shame.

It seemed his father's very life was leaving him with every labored breath. Finally, with herculean effort, he managed to whisper, "I'm sorry, son. I...I tried. Never m-mea—"

The man wheezed, convulsed, and his chest depressed one last time.

A doctor and Mr. Wiggin's nurse rushed into the room, having heard Wendell's fearful cry.

"What happened?" the doctor asked, as he rushed to the patient's side.

Glancing momentarily over his shoulder at the candlelit corner where the unnamable apparition had taken form only moments ago, Wendell said, "I was sitting here by his side, and he became gray and had trouble breathing. Before I knew it, he clutched his chest, shuddered twice, and that was it. It was over that quick. I never even had a chance to say goodbye."

"I'm so sorry for your loss," the nurse said with more affection than her appearance would betray. She momentarily put a comforting hand on his shoulder, as all there stared at the body in silence; but as quickly as the sympathetic gestures appeared, they once more hid themselves behind those beady dark eyes, and her cold professionalism took over. The nurse said matter-of-factly to the doctor, "I'll send for Father Casey, then I'll return to start preparing the body."

She then excused herself from the room.

"A priest?" Wendell queried in vexation. "Again with the spiritual fascinations. When did my father become a religious man?"

"You will have to ask his associate outside for that information," the doctor said, as he pulled the covers up over the dead man's head. "The first thing he said when we admitted him was that when he died, we were to call on Father Casey. He had made all arrangements for burial with St. Patrick's Catholic Church. In fact, he must have known his time was close; the priest was just here not but an hour and a quarter before you arrived to give Last Rites to the man."

The doctor turned to depart the room. "I'll leave you to say your goodbyes."

Wendell stopped him before he disappeared beyond the door. "Doctor, what, exactly, was wrong with my father?"

He cleared his throat, seemed almost embarrassed to admit, "Your father was cleared in every test we performed. As far as could be told, there was absolutely nothing wrong with the man other than he was perpetually sleep deprived for a reason we could not put a finger to. You see the manifestation of that," he said, sweeping an arm around the room full of lights. He rubbed his jaw perplexed. "I'll put down on his death certificate that he died of an unknown paroxysm. I'm sorry that we weren't more help to him."

The doctor then closed the door behind him as he left room.

Wendell looked down on his lifeless father under the white sheet then over at the corner of the room where something had become alive in the shadows left by the extinguished candles. A snake of apprehension slithered up his back and sunk its teeth into the nape of his neck, making his hair stand on end.

"I doubt anyone in medicine could have helped cure what killed my father," he whispered.

2

Wendell and Arnold sat in somber silence on the hillside outside Hamot Hospital, looking out over the bay and Presque Ilse beyond. White triangular sails gamboled across its surface. They skirted alongside a multitude of fishing boats and the steamer taking patrons to the Massassauga Point Hotel on the flats where the peninsula connected to the mainland.

Wendell picked at the browning grass absentmindedly, as he took in the view. "I've forgotten how nice it is here along the lakeshore," he said. "I tend to spend my time now in the south of Erie, maybe travel down to Waterford on occasion."

"You loved it here," Arnold reminisced. "Mr. Wiggins could never get you off the peninsula as a boy. What's made you stay away for so long? There can't have been much to do in the country."

"Oh, I have my hobbies —"

" —Yes, I've seen your hobbies —"

" —But I mostly was just trying to stay out of Father's way. It's no secret that I was a disappointment to him. He only proved my point when he tossed me from the house."

"The disappointment that got you tossed from the house was a genuine frustration on your father's part. You had an opportunity to be a responsible man and you chose not to."

""Yes, well we don't need to rehash that at the moment," Wendell interjected.

Going on Arnold said, "I think the general disappointment *you* are referring to was misplaced. I could tell something had been eating at him from very early on. A secret of some sort that he would not betray. It started shortly after you mother died."

They were silent but only for a moment, for Wendell decided to use that last statement to open the door to the topic he really wanted to discuss. He was hoping to pry information from Arnold that his father had no time to divulge.

Feeling out the extent of Arnold's knowledge Wendell asked, "What was the purpose for all the lit candles in father's room? That request must have seemed peculiar."

Arnold rubbed his big scruffy chin. "Now that's an oddity that's right hard to explain. Mr. Wiggins had that peculiarity a long time ago—when you were a boy—for the better part of a year. Then, as quickly as it started it stopped, but his mood changed permanently and not for the good. That orneriness is what you remember. Even after he stopped lighting all the candles at night, he still feared the dark. That never seemed to go away. Then about, oh I'd say the last year, I think, he started doing it all over again." He knitted his brow and scratched at the bald spot on his head contemplatively in silence, as if trying his best to recall and give as accurate an account as possible. After a moment he then added, "Well, I'm not sure exactly when it started up again, but it was sometime after you left—"

"—Kicked out," Wendell corrected. "Did he ever give a reason for it?" he then pressed.

A cloud of seagulls cawed in the distance, as they swooped and swirled above a newly docked fishing boat. The smell of fish, even at the distance of a several hundred feet was noticeable in the cool, fall air.

"Not to me," Arnold finally said with a note of frustration. "He was very secretive about what afflicted him. He never talked about why he hated the dark so much.

Why he insisted on sleeping in the light. And it got worse towards the end. Kept the whole house lit all the time, lamps and candles everywhere. Surprised the damned place didn't burn to the ground. Then he got to the point where he wasn't sleeping at all. He got weak and funny acting. That's when I brought him here. In the end, I think that's what killed him—lack of sleep."

Wendell thought back to the shadowy adumbration that struggled in the corner of the hospital room. The thought of those sickly sour-yellow eyes staring at him and what would have happened if he hadn't relit the candles…He understood completely why his father feared the dark.

Realizing that Arnold seemed to possess less knowledge of the strange events than did Wendell, he decided to act upon an idea that he'd been entertaining since his father's last breath.

"I believe you're going to have to stay here and prepare things with the priest that's coming?" Wendell asked.

"The next few days are going to be busy ones for me and the household to get things ready for the funeral,"

Arnold agreed, as he extracted his behemoth frame from the grassy hillside.

"Am I still banned from the house?"

Arnold sighed. Wendell could tell he was conflicted. "Even now, you are still considered the prodigal son out in the world, penniless and — hopefully — penitent. I'm fairly certain that your circumstances will change for the better once the will is read, but it must remain so until then."

"So yes, then?"

"Yes. You are still banned from the house."

"Is there at least anything I can do to help?"

Digging into his pocket, Arnold pulled out some money held in a bundle with a silver clip and, handing it to Wendell, said, "Mr. Wiggins had everything spelled out in great detail what each of our duties were to be upon his death." He plunked the money into Wendell's hand. "Yours is to buy some decent clothes, get a hotel room on the Diamond and wait. I'll come fetch you for the viewing and funeral. The reading of the will comes a day or two after."

Looking over the money Wendell said, "There's well more here than what I would need for a change of clothes and a room."

"Then give some of it to Verity. She has two of your children to raise."

With that, the big man lumbered back up to the hospital, and Wendell was left there on that little hill in silent humiliation.

· · · · ·

South from the lakefront, Wendell ambled deep in thought. If it weren't for his father's remarks, which had made him realize the elder Wiggins was seeing the same thing he was, he'd swear he was hallucinating the thing in the shadows. He was very practiced at hallucination; they were his constant companions while high on opium. Those hallucinations were mostly idyllic ones, however. Not ones that looked as though they crawled up from the very pit of hell. One reverie of that nature would have broken him from that habit before it ever started.

He had decided to reconnoiter the elder Wiggins' bedroom. It had been his sanctuary from the world of lies, deceit, and backstabbing that had become a part of a business Wendell could not bring himself to be a part of (horseshoe manufacturing was more ruthless than one would imagine on the surface of it). If Father held any secrets they would most likely be found somewhere in that room.

A few blocks up was the Diamond. It was a large public park now bustling with chatting mothers with their prams and lounge-abouts. The park was often full, especially now with warm color raining down from every tree at the slightest breeze. They came to see this display and to get in as much sun and fresh air before the harsh Great Lakes winter settled over the area in the next month and a half.

Wendell followed the park's perimeter, turned west, crossed Peach Street, and hastened down West 6th Street.

West 6th Street, also known as "Millionaire's Row", was filled with the grandest architecture that Erie's business barons could buy. They ranged from great gray granite, to brick, to glimmering alabaster wood, but all had one thing in common: they all tried to outdo their neighbor in grandiosity. Some had large Romanesque columns, others had great mullioned windows and intricately manicured lawns; all had carriage houses as large as barns.

The elder Wiggins was not quite in this league, but it wasn't for a lack of trying. His home was a slightly-less-grand, many-gabled brick house at the corner of West 6th and Holland Streets—the caboose of the train of mansions. It was nestled on a large wooded lot surrounded by old, shady elms and white oaks and sugar maples, all dropping their leaves in a hurricane of reds and browns and yellows. The house looked no different from his last memory of it, though there seemed to be some moss growing on the roof at one corner. It must have been a recent development, for the persnickety elder Wiggins would never have allowed such a blemish and had it rectified at once with much consternation.

Wendell knew he couldn't just walk nonchalantly into his old home. Sully—Jack Sullivan, Mr. Wiggins' Butler, would never let him pass without Mr. Wiggins—and now Arnold's—express consent. He decided it more prudent to take a more surreptitious route into his father's house.

He turned north on Holland and walked until the carriage house was between himself and the dwelling. Then, using stealth, Wendell slalomed from tree to tree until he came to the one he wanted: an old white oak that stretched fifty feet into the fall sky with thick, octopus-like branches.

With mature Rhododendrons along the sides of the house and the mammoth trunk to shield him, he would only be visible for the last few feet of his climb until he came to his father's bedroom. As long as the window was not latched, he could gain entrance, although he still wasn't sure what he would be looking for once he was inside.

Verifying that no one was about to see his climb, Wendell slowly and surreptitiously ascended the outstretched limbs.

Everything transpired as Wendell had hoped, and he now found himself in his father's bedroom. It was now approaching noon. Sully and Mrs. Sully, the cook, and Miss Betty, the maid, would all be down in the basement quarters eating lunch. Wendell suspected he had half-hour before they returned to their tasks, and he'd more than likely be found out and tossed out on his ear.

He looked around the great room. As suspected, candelabras and oil lamps occupied almost every empty space. However cluttered it may have been, it was still spotless, and the candelabras and oil lamps were set out as if on some grand display; a testament that even without the elder Wiggins home, his ire was still feared.

Wendell's attention was immediately drawn to the great chest of drawers along the far wall. Along the top were photographs, papers, ledgers, and books with an oval mirror placed strategically in the middle. Strewn in between were lamps and candles, some waxy nubs in dire need of being replaced.

This was as good a place to start as any.

He quietly tip-toed to the chiffonier and began moving things about looking for something he, as yet, did not know. He poked around the papers, all business of one sort or another. Father had left his gold pocket watch behind when he had taken ill. This Wendell put in his front pocket without a second thought, as he picked up and perused the photographs—mostly of Mother before she died. One was of his parents together outside the newly expanded factory. They looked happy.

But there was one in particular that caught his eye: to the right of the mirror was a small picture of Wendell in a brass frame. It was of him at Presque Ilse as an adolescent fishing in the waters of the bay. He was surprised that Father even tolerated this picture, let alone felt compelled to display it openly. Wendell was certain that when he was evicted from the home all traces of him would have been exorcised, as well.

It was only when he was about to replace it next to the mirror that he realized his hand was beginning to visibly shake. He tried to play the tremor off as nervousness of possibly being caught, however, he knew the symptom well. He did his best to ignore it—for the time being, anyway. He knew from experience that he couldn't disregard it for long.

Another minute of shuffling through the contents on the chest of drawers revealed nothing of any significance to his search.

He next searched the wardrobe, but that, too, was fruitless.

Wendell was about to inspect the space under his father's bed when an unexpected noise from downstairs drew his attention away from his exploration. He could hear a door creak open and the old servant couple bickering—something about too much salt on the perch. Miss Betty vehemently disagreed (she did everything with vehemence).

Wendell cursed under his breath; they were done with lunch early and were beginning the afternoon phase of their daily sacramental — they would go through each room one by one to make sure no dirt or dust had settled on what they had vigorously cleaned in the morning. They would soon be upstairs. They always started on the top floor, usually in Father's bedroom, and worked their way back downstairs.

Wendell hastily retraced his steps to the window, quietly reclosed it once outside, and descended the old oak to the safety of the yard below, cursing the entire way at coming away with no better an idea of what that dark monstrosity was that had directly or indirectly killed his father.

3

Wendell walked into the Reed House hotel like he owned it. He strode with confidence over the polished floor to the wall length, mahogany counter and said to the well-coiffed desk clerk, "I'd like a room, please."

The desk clerk eyed Wendell suspiciously, looked him up and down, taking in his shabby appearance. "I think you want the Clarendon down by the docks."

His face gleamed with a wry smile. "No, no, my good man. This will do just fine."

He pulled out the money Arnold had given him and waved it in the young man's face. "I'll be here for a while, but I'll pay for just three days in advance. Give it a bit of a go to see if it's worth any more than that," he teased. "If not, I may have to try the Ellesworth down the way."

The desk clerk sighed in exasperation, as he eyed the money being waved about. "Sir, may I suggest that if you are going to stay here that you at least . . . update your wardrobe?"

"Part of my master plan, you see, but first things first: I need a room in which to *put* my new wardrobe."

As Wendell signed in the hotel registry, the desk clerk pulled a key from a mahogany wall behind him. "May I suggest McWilliams Clothier next door?" he advocated, as he handed Wendell the key.

Wendell handed him three days' payment. "You may. And I will, thank you."

With a tangled look on his face, the clerk was about to say something but stopped short.

Reading that querying expression, Wendell said as he turned to leave, "I was thrown into a water trough. Don't tell me that's never happened to you."

. . . . .

Wendell bought three changes of clothes, washed up and, thus looking like a proper gentleman, now lay on the bed in his hotel room, looking like a well-dressed ass, as he picked at some fuzz on his newly-creased pant leg. A loud sigh filled the room. He had failed at finding anything of note in his father's house and was now unsure of what to do or what to think, which was rather disappointing. A sleuth he was not.

What had transpired in his father's hospital room was otherworldly. Things don't just materialize from thin air. Yet he was as sure as rain on Sunday that what he saw was not a figment of his imagination. He was also fairly certain that shadows don't move about on their own, and they certainly don't have the capacity for seeing. Yet that shadow in the room roiled like bubbling tar, and its jaundiced eyes — eyes that should not have been there — peered right at him, almost seeming to look into his very being. He didn't believe in hocus pocus religious tomfoolery. Yet...

With no conscious thought, Wendell suddenly leapt from the bed and raced to the window overlooking the Diamond. His hands now trembled terribly, as he tried without success to gain access to fresh air. His mouth seemed lined with cotton when he tried to lick his dried lips back to life. An anxiety had abruptly overtaken him. It wasn't an apprehension born from fear, necessarily, though fear, no doubt, was a component. No, this was his body's way of saying it needed more opium. As his body got used to the drug, it craved it more and more to acquire the same level of bliss Wendell couldn't attain in any attempt at a normal life.

He sighed, for he always—and usually gladly—fed that hunger. He would have to now, as well, if for no other reason than to keep his body satisfied while he tried to figure out what it was he saw in his father's room.

Wendell turned from the window, as he flexed his shaking hands in an attempt at calming them, grabbed the remaining money from the night stand next to him, and headed to a place known to only a few and attended by still less.

. . . .

At the east end of the docks along the shores of the bay was a line of fishing supply shops. The last establishment in this line was a nondescript structure, much the same as the rest. Its only difference was a solid door instead of a glass front and no windows.

A wooden walkway serviced these small establishments, and it was in dire need of repair. Wendell mooched carefully along, making sure he stepped precisely, fearing a misstep would cause a spill and the ruination of his new clothes.

A line of small boats tapped an odd syncopation against their moorings, as waves lapped between them along the shoreline to his left.

After winding his way along the water-warped, splintered boardwalk, Wendell stopped at the last door, hesitated briefly, and knocked.

A small rectangular opening appeared and two dark, glassy eyes stared out at him. "What you want? We closed," said a squeaky, oriental voice on the other side.

Wendell replied, "I find myself in dire need to chase the dragon."

The eyes bounced left then right nervously. "We no do that here. Go away."

The man on the other side of the door was about to close the peep hole when Wendell pulled out his money and waved it in front of him. "I regularly chase at Imau's down on Parade, but I find myself here at the moment."

"No like Imau. He take business from me."

"Then consider me *restitution*," Wendell replied with a smile.

The two beady eyes looked around again from their peep hole. The money finally won out over trepidation. "Fine. You come in. Quickly, quickly."

When Wendell slipped inside the door, the man relocked it behind him and led him past fishing supplies to a back room behind the counter. He could see why this establishment was losing out over Imau's. It was a small, dirty room. The walls were stained with smoke residue, and no pictures or tapestries adorned them, as they did at Imau's. Three threadbare couches in a U shape around a long rectangular table were fixed on the left side of the room. There was a lit oil lamp in the center of the table with opium pipes placed all around. These were currently being used by slovenly men, all at or near unconsciousness.

At the other end of the room were three tattered rugs, ill-lit by candlelight. Two men were inhaling deeply from their pipes, one rug and pipe lay empty. The little oriental man pointed to it. "You sit there. All ready to go. You pay me now."

Wendell paid the man, sat at his rug and lit his pipe. Soon, he was feeling much the way he'd felt before Arnold had so rudely awakened him from his reverie earlier in the day. He felt light, calm, and his body tingled in that funny way it does when the opium takes effect.

His first hazy thoughts, like heat-induced ripples off a summer macadam, were of Verity and the twins, little Abel and Becca — his would be family. The guilt he carried of his absence from them was monumental. He had never wanted to leave them. He wanted even more to be that man that Arnold had said he refused to be. Just as he did with his father, he cared for them and loved them. He somehow just didn't feel worthy of them. It was an emptiness he had carried about for as long as he could remember, like a great weight that constantly tried to pull him under the waves of irrelevance.

Then *poof*, they were gone, evaporated into the air like the smoke that escaped his inhalations.

Next was his mother: her sandy, wild curls; her ever-present smile that stretched into forever; her hugs, so strong he thought he'd be smothered in their embraces, yet that strength was more soothing than anything he could put into words.

Then *poof*, she was gone, as well.

Lastly was his father, however these thoughts were not fond memories of halcyon days but more recent in origin: they were of the hospital room earlier in the day. His recollection now, though, was slightly different than what had actually transpired. When his father had told him to dowse the candles in his hand, every wick in the room lost its flame. He was plunged into darkness. A darkness so complete that one would think that light did not — could not — exist in the void around him.

Wendell called out to his father but the silence in return was deafening. Wherever the light went, sound seemed to follow behind like an obedient dog.

Out of the empty silence something thick, cold, and wet locked around his neck, cutting off a scream. He found himself suddenly off his feet and landing on an icy, hard surface that knocked the wind from him.

This was like no other opium dream Wendell had ever experienced. The fear he felt seemed real, not imagined. The pain he now felt was very real.

A light that had no origin appeared above like a spotlight, shining down on him. Nothing about his surroundings, however, came into focus.

He had somehow lost his new clothes and now lie naked, outstretched on a cold, slick slab of waist-high stone. The chain linked cuff around his neck made it almost impossible to breath, and now cuffs materialized around his feet and wrists, as well. These, however, seemed laced with barbs for they cut into his skin. Drops of blood dripped into the grave-dark spaces beyond his peripheral vision.

"Hello, Mr. Wiggins," came a voice from the shadows. It seemed everywhere but nowhere. It was deep, gravelly, cumbersome, as though it had more teeth than could fit in its mouth. It spoke slowly, with deliberation, in a decidedly alien inflection "We finally meet. Your father told me many things about you, which made me long for this moment."

He struggled in the chains to no avail. His head throbbed mightily and the back of it felt sticky. His racing heart exacerbated the pain. "What do you want?" he cried out.

"For the moment just to enjoy this."

Another chain propelled forward from the shadows by an unseen force. At its end was a large, razor-tipped hook. Before Wendell had time to react to its presence, the hook lodged itself into then through his left side and pulled itself taught, stretching his skin. Blood pooled in the puncture then spidered down his side.

Wendell screamed in agony. He wanted to struggle to free himself, but he already felt as though he was stretched to the point of being torn apart.

As the thing in the shadows laughed, a grotesque, phlegmy gurgle, a second hooked chain flew from the shadows and lodged itself in Wendell's other side, stretching his skin to the point of tearing.

He cried out a second time, face contorted in an admixture of excruciating pain and abject terror.

"Please! Please stop!" Wendell begged between struggled breaths. "Wh-what do you want from me?"

"I'm old," it said mockingly. "I get very little enjoyment in my old age. Let me partake in this one small pleasure first then we shall chat."

The inky space to his right began to churn, like boiling pitch. From within this slithering mass, sickly yellow eyes suddenly materialized. Wendell recognized them—they were the eyes from his father's hospital room.

The formless mass began to take shape as it inched toward the light. Wendell tried to blink back a pain that put him on the verge of unconsciousness. He could not force his eyes into focus, but the thing had a definite humanoid form. He could make out through blurred vision a massive body with bosselated outlines.

The creature stopped just on the perimeter of the cone of light. Its unblinking eyes looked him up and down, seemed to be considering Wendell's predicament with sadistic intent.

Suddenly, the stone platform he had been laying on was gone, and he remained in position only by the cuffs and hooks in his side.

Wendell screamed impossibly louder, as the tension became almost too much to bare. Blood streamed from each wound as punctures stretched and barbs cut deeper. He screamed and screamed.

Still staying within the shadows, the thing slowly walked the perimeter around Wendell's outstretched body. It whispered in low tones — which sounded not unlike the buzz of angry hornets — a language that Wendell did not know. When it reached Wendell's head it lowered itself while still staying hidden in sepulchral darkness and whispered, "Now we shall talk."

Blinking back tears, Wendell stuttered, "Wh-what is it y-you want from me?"

"I want you children. Give me your children and your suffering will stop."

Without warning, all the chains retracted back into the darkness with the force of being pulled by draught horses, ripping skin and dislocating joints, before several *pops* sent Wendell into a cold, quiet blackness.

4

"Hey. Hey! You scaring the customers!"

Wendell shot up from his nightmare to the little oriental man angrily shaking his shoulder.

"You go. You scare the customers."

Wendell reflexively felt around his neck, as he tried to calm his hyperventilating breaths. He then moved quickly to his arms and legs—all intact. He pulled up his shirt and looked at his sides, expecting puncture wounds from the hooks, but there was no sign at all that he'd been impaled.

Wendell looked around the room. All eyes were on him, all tinged with dope-mingled fear.

"You go now. No more," implored the little man as his pulled Wendell up to his feet. "The dragon no like you."

Still trying to shake off the high, not sure what had just transpired, not sure what was happening now, he staggered forward at the firm insistence of the store owner, who seemed stronger than his stature would suggest.

Before Wendell had a chance to even form a reply or rebuttal, he was back outside, and the door slammed closed behind him.

Trying to rub sobriety back into his eyes, Wendell looked around him to see if anyone had seen the abrupt display. Boats were meandering back to the docks, and those that had already made it in were too busy buttoning up and taking inventory to take any notice of him. At the moment, he was the only one on the bay front not engaged in some sort of meaningful undertaking.

Noticing the sun bleeding onto the treetops to the west, Wendell figured it was nearing 6:00 p.m. That meant it would be dark soon. Having seen what the thing could do in his dreams, he was in no hurry to see what it would do in the coming darkness.

He picked through the rotting walkway faster on the return trip, not caring about whether or not he took a spill. He needed to get to his room and get it lit.

As he rushed back up the hill to his hotel room, Wendell began to favor his sides; though no wounds were present, they still pinched painfully.

· · · · ·

The desk clerk was thumbing through the newspaper when Wendell rushed up to the counter. "Can I send a message over to St. Patrick's and have Father, uh, what's his name—"

"Casey," the clerk interjected, not looking up from his reading.

"—yeah, Casey. Can you send him a telegram to have him come over here, to my room in 313? Wendell Wiggins. He'll know the name, I believe. The last name, anyway. It's urgent."

Glancing up only momentarily to make sure the interlocutor wasn't kidding, the desk clerk offered, "You do realize the church is literally just two blocks away," and resumed his reading.

"Yes, but it's getting dark out."

The clerk's paper perusal stopped, if only for a moment, as Wendell gave his rejoinder. He never looked up, only stared blankly at the newsprint, as if trying to process how a lack of light had any bearing on the church's location. Not finding an adequate response to this, the desk clerk's head resumed its slight back and forth motion as it followed his eyes along the page without offering up a reply.

"I'll pay for the telegram," Wendell added, as he reached into the inner pocket of his suitcoat — and realized his clip and the money it held was missing.

"Sonofabitch!" he cursed under his breath, as he checked his other pockets to no avail. The thieving, little china man must have removed it from his pocket when he was being ripped apart in his opium dream.

Yet another reason people were going to Imau's to get high.

"Never mind," Wendell said as he rushed back across the large foyer to the double front doors of the hotel.

The clerk looked back up from his paper, watching Wendell run. He repeated to himself with a note of confusion, "It's only two blocks away. Literally. Two blocks."

He shook his head disparagingly and returned to his paper.

· · · · ·

The sky was a deep blue, bruising to purple, but there was still enough light to cast long shadows that stretched across the walkway. However, in the deeper shadows, between houses or the inky spaces between closely spaced trees, the darkness moved. Wendell could see it come alive from the corners of his eyes. It writhed like slow-moving lava, but he kept up his run, stumbling occasionally over an upheaved brick or root peeking between them. If he stayed within the lighter spaces he figured he'd be safe — but not for much longer.

Finally, at the corner of East Fourth and Holland Streets stood St. Patrick's Roman Catholic Church, its brick edifice stained in the twilight.

Wendell would have to have some words with that desk clerk when he returned; it was actually four blocks, not two.

He climbed the steep steps two at a time, opened, then disappeared, behind the large wooden doors.

Never having been in a church of any variety, Wendell went where instinct told him. He saw flickering light through the archway of the narthex and quickly crossed it and ran down the center isle of the nave. The left of the altar was alight with a massive display of votive candles arranged in a semi-circle around a white marble statue of the Blessed Virgin.

Sitting in the front pew, directly in front of the statue, with a broom at his side, was a priest about a decade older than Wendell by appearance. He had squared features and dark, wavy hair, sliced here and there with a thread of gray. He seemed deep in thought and didn't at first notice Wendell as he rounded the row of pews.

"Hello," Wendell said. "I'm looking for Father Casey. You him?"

The priest crossed himself as he rose and greeted Wendell with a warm smile and bright, enthusiastic eyes. "I am," he said, taking Wendell's hand in a vigorous shake. "Who do I have the pleasure of speaking to?" He was also a tall man, and hidden under his cassock must have been a bale of muscles for his grip was a solid, almost painful, one. "Forgive me. You don't look like any of my parishioners."

"No forgiveness needed. I don't go to church here."

"Oh, where do you worship?"

"I don't."

The priest's earnest smile only became wider, "Well, some people liken the church to a hospital. They only go when they are spiritually ill. So what ails you?"

"I believe you know, er knew, my father, William Wiggins."

The priest was hesitant before he answered. "Yes. You must be Alastair then—oh wait; it is Wendell, now, is it not?"

"Yes, Wendell, Wendell Wiggins. I go by my middle name now. Long story."

"Yes, your father apprised me," he assured Wendell as he motioned for them to sit, and they resumed their conversation in the silent stare of the alabaster Virgin.

"I am very sorry for your loss," Father Casey started. "For the short time I knew him, he seemed a very nice man."

"Are you sure we're talking about the same person?" Wendell quipped.

"Oh, I know he seemed gruff and somewhat off-putting at times, if I may say that—"

"You may."

"—but he really did mean well, for all his faults."

"Yes, I'm sure he did mean well," Wendell retorted, "but not all he did actually turned out well." He then eyed fretfully the emergent gloom, like an alien mold, crawling up the wall and along the isles of the church.

"Forgiveness is a wonderful elixir for ill feelings," the priest offered.

"It is not forgiveness I'm seeking at the moment—it's answers. Answers to things I've seen today. Answers to things that I've had done to me that I cannot explain, not naturally, anyway."

He stopped momentarily to look around him once again. Something was close by. He could feel its stare, though the glowing, putrid eyes could not be readily identified. He then continued, "My father wasn't a religious man, yet he came to you. I, in desperation, am following in his footsteps." He hesitated only a moment then revealed, "There was something in my father's room when he died. Something I cannot describe and certainly do not understand."

At that revelation, and before Wendell could elaborate further—though he really wasn't sure how that elaboration would take form—the priest's features darkened into something that seemed foreign to his face. It was as though his muscles puckered into positions unnatural for them. He held up a finger, telling Wendell he wanted to do something before he answered.

The priest went into a small room between the statue and the altar and came back a moment later with more candles. He then lit them from the candles around the statue and set them in the pews all around them. Within a few minutes their end of the church was a conflagration of light and flame.

When the priest sat back down he said, "Does that answer your question? Your father came to me in late winter and articulated this whole ghastly affair to me."

"And you believed him? Just like that?"

"No, no, not at first. Many supposed supernatural things can have very natural explanations."

"Did you see it yourself? Did you see the thing in the shadows?"

"No. He tried to show me. It didn't—or wouldn't—manifest itself to me."

"Yet you still believed him?"

"I only had to see the look of terror on his face to know he was seeing something. Something very real to him, even if I couldn't see it. Yet in my line of work, you don't need to see evil to know it's there. It can manifest itself in so many ways. In his case it was his sleeplessness and paranoia to the darkness. A possession of sorts but like no other possession I have ever read about or seen."

"So in the end, there was really nothing you could do to help him?"

The priest's blue eyes wandered over to the glimmering, snowy marble of the Blessed Mother. There was a sense of failure in them. "No, and I can't tell you how sorry I am that I couldn't. His fate was sealed long before he ever sought me out. In the end, all I could do was help prepare him for what was to come."

He then firmly fixed his gaze back onto Wendell. "But you . . . Your father told me about how he passed this affliction onto you, as well. I was going to search you out tomorrow. I may still have time to help you, if the Lord wills it."

"For the sake of argument how about we just assume he does."

Suddenly, there was a noise hidden in the gloom on the opposite end of the altar—a slow, scratchy clatter that reverberated off the stone and stained glass.

Wendell turned so fast he thought his neck would snap. His heart felt like it was going to tear through its cage of bone, and it was though his very breath was in terror, for it refused to leave his body, clinging painfully in his throat. He reflexively moved away from the noise in the dark, almost knocking Father Casey from the pew behind him.

Suddenly, from within the inky shadows where the candlelight could not penetrate, an old, withered man on unstable feet shuffled into the light, wearing similar garb in which the young priest was attired. "Father Casey, your supper is getting cold. I thought you'd be done long before now. You know the rule: we eat together."

"Sorry, Monsignor Thomas. I was just saying a little prayer to the Blessed Mother before coming in when this gentleman, Mr. Wendell Wiggins, William Wiggins' son, came in for some consoling words; as you know Mr. Wiggins died today."

"Well, supper waits for no one. Do you think Jesus waited on the Apostles at the Last Supper while they gabbed with the Pharisees out in the street? Come, come. And what's with all the candles? This is how you run your parish—wasting candles like this. The Church isn't made of money, you know. Blow them out and come to supper."

To Wendell he said, "Young man, I'm sorry for your loss. I knew your father. Good business man. We have Mass in the morning at 7:00 a.m. I suggest you get your consoling then."

He then wobbled and trundled his way back into the darkness.

Wendell looked upon Father Casey with brow askew, to which the priest replied, "Don't let his tone fool you. He's well meaning. He's just so long in the tooth he's forgotten how to show it."

"Maybe he and my dear old dad are related."

The priest rose from the pew and grabbed a couple glass votives and handed them to Wendell. "I hope this is enough light to get you back home without incident. I have to do the morning Mass, but can I call upon you afterwards? I can share with you then the things I've been able to uncover, however little it has been. It is only a start, but every journey, no matter how short or how long, has to start with a first step."

"You can't divulge your findings now?" Wendell asked anxiously.

"I don't have time, now. If I'm not in there to eat my cold supper in the next few minutes, I won't eat again for four days. That's my penance for not being to supper on time."

"I take it it's happened before."

"Only once, and I wish it to never happen again. Monsignor takes his meals very seriously. Although this is my parish, he is a guest here. He is a senior priest, and I need to give him the respect he deserves, however much it may pain me."

Father Casey paused a moment, as if in reflection on what he was about to say. He then added, "Monsignor is dying. He has a cancer on his legs he acquired when on a missionary trip to the tropics. The ulcers are spreading. So, if sitting together with him at supper comforts him, then I will sit with him every night till God takes him home. I know I ask a lot of you when I ask only for this one night, but I am only one man and others need me, as well."

The priest's expression turned serious. "Will you be alright till tomorrow morning? Can you stay awake?"

Wendell shrugged. "I don't know that I have a choice. It won't be my first all-nighter, but it'll be the first I've attempted sober."

"Good. Where shall I call at?"

"The Reed House, room 313."

The priest started rounding up the votive candles he took from the room, quickly blowing them out one by one. As he did so, and before Wendell turned to leave, Father Casey said, "I will tell you this one thing, and it will have to suffice till tomorrow: if you find yourself in the company of this evil, what it does to you, as real as it may seem and feel, is only an illusion. That, I only know because of what your father had already relayed to me in our conversations together. Whatever it does to you will not kill you. It wants something from you and cannot get it if you are dead."

Wendell replied pensively, "It has already revealed its demand—my children."

Father Casey made a sign of the cross and said, "Then God be with your children, my friend. And whatever you do, whatever it does to you, *do not* consent when it asks for them. Do you understand? Any assent on your part, however slight, is all the license it needs, and their fates will be sealed."

"That is the one thing about this whole affair that I *do* understand."

"Good. I'll see you in the morning."

5

Wendell opened up the church doors to a landscape that had been hungrily consumed by the night. The moon hung shyly just below the tree line, as if worried it might be the next course, keeping the gloom thick.

His two flickers of salvation delicately danced on either side of him, as he took his first apprehensive steps away from what strangely felt like a place of refuge.

The first block was traversed without incident. He constantly took in his surroundings in an anxious dread, peering into the blackest crevasses. Movement was felt more than seen, as the ring of light surrounding him kept him in a cocoon of safety.

As the hushed desolation of the house-lined street began to give way to small shops, some still open and alight a block and a half from the hotel, Wendell dared to breathe a sigh of relief. In many spots, the lights from the shops outshined his candles and if it weren't for an ever-present fear of being drawn and quartered, he would have, if even briefly, considered extinguishing his own candles.

Then it happened. He stumbled on a root along a footpath between two darkened properties. Wendell caught himself before the stagger became a fall, but in righting himself, both candles were extinguished.

The tenebrous night to his right began to yawn awake. Wicked whispers caressed Wendell's ears while he desperately searched for an ignition source to relight his candles. He quickly realized that there were none, but before the thought of running became a reality, something from the shadows snatched him and pulled him into its onyx embrace.

Roiling all around him, like thunder clouds on a moonless night, a pall dropped over Erie. Wendell was not only alone, he seemed void even of a firmament, suspended in a heavy broth of nothingness with those manic susurrations confessing an evil he could not understand.

His eyes became cataract, his heart hammered so violently that he felt certain that it would detonate within his chest. He could feel its pounding in every limb as he floated in that black soup.

Then, slowly around him there came vague suggestions of substance. His feet stretched impossibly at it, hoping something firm would reciprocate the reach.

At once, it was as if someone turned the lights back on. Wendell found himself prostrate inside a hollowed piece of metal, its volume only about twice Wendell's size. His heavy breaths echoed off its brass-colored walls.

"I missed you," came the filthy voice from somewhere to his right outside his containment. "I was so hoping you would stay and play some more." Suddenly, the thing's grotesquely slurred voice was now at his left. "But all is well, now. You have returned. Shall we resume playing?"

"You are not getting what you asked for," Wendell cried out. "I will never give up my children. Do to me what you will."

"And I shall. We have ample time, for eternity is pregnant with it. Make no mistake. I will get what I want. Did you know it took your father nearly a year of my company before he finally gave you up? He was a strong-willed man, stronger than most. I suspect it will take decidedly less time than that before you will be willing to give up the entirety of the world to make the pain stop."

Wendell was surprised at the revelation. Not so much of his father's admission that he had given Wendell over to a demon; the confession was self-explanatory, if not wholly unbelievable at the time. He was more surprised that his father would endure a year of tormented afflictions of unimaginable pain to try and save his son. He had always thought his father held an untold disappointment or even dislike of him; but if that were so, why did the elder Wiggins not give Wendell up right away to stop the torment? Maybe his father had cared for him more than he realized.

Wendell unbuttoned the collar of his shirt, as the temperature in the metal entrapment began to warm. He began to squirm uncomfortably.

"If I am to do my job properly," the voice went on," I need to know what makes you tick, since we are only newly acquainted." Something like bony pincers clicked excitedly. "Let me ask, if I may be so bold as to do so, what scares you? What things — *terrify* you?"

"Big breasted, bare naked blonds," Wendell quipped. "Scared to death of them."

"Ah, a sense of humor in the face of adversity."

"I got that from my mother."

"Your father was rather a dry and direct person, I admit. Your torment might be more enjoyable than I first thought."

Wendell adjusted himself in the oddly-shaped enclosure, and it was then, when he felt the heat radiating from underneath him, that he began to take in his surroundings with more scrutiny. The walls rolled up and around at odd angles and at one end, the end he was facing, it narrowed severely with two small holes burrowing to unknown places at its most contracted point.

Now the mucoid slur of odd intonation was all around him, echoing off the brass walls in every direction, as it said, "I will endeavor not to disappoint you in my attempt at your suffering. I never have to look far when I try to realize new and different ways of instilling it. Man, since time immemorial, has had an uncanny way of knowing just the right way of inflicting pain upon his fellow man. It is an odd concoction—pain and terror—and just the right proportions distills the most gratifying drink. It is an aptitude I am surprised your god befitted you with but a gift I am only happy to replicate."

The heat was becoming unbearable. Wendell's clothes were swiftly becoming saturated with sweat. He could no longer touch the metal's surface. Even his clothing was no longer a barrier. He struggled to a crouching position with his knees tucked up to his chest so at least the thicker soles of his shoes would provide a brief respite.

It was in this crouching position that he noticed the metal underneath him began to take on a different color.

Wendell, with quick repetitions, beat upon the sides, only to have his hands burned in the attempt.

The voice outside again said, "I was there when Perillos of Athens created this wonderful piece. It's always been a personal favorite of mine."

"What are you doing to me?" Wendell pleaded. "What contraption do you have me in?" He tried to move, but the soles of his shoes were beginning to smoke and adhere to the now glowing metal. The heated air was nothing compared to the scorching knives of pain now beginning to stab up through the soles his feet.

"Have you ever heard of the Bronze Bull? No, probably not; education isn't what is should be. You are inside a hollowed out bronze bull under which a fire has been lit."

Wendell shifted, but his feet did not move, making him lose his balance. He fell to his right, and his arm was immediately seared. He pushed himself upright as he cried out, but the agony lingered. His shirt was charred and burned away, while the skin underneath was beet-red and bubbling.

Now, even the air was so hot Wendell's lungs burned with every breath.

The orange-red bronze beneath him began to transform to yellow-white.

Wendell screamed in agony, however every inhalation of the super-heated air only made it harder to breathe.

"All you have to do is say yes," the voice said. "Yes is such a simple word. Even near death anyone can manage a *yes*. I say again, give me your children."

"Y-y," Wendell stuttered, as he tried to release his burning feet from the melted shoes.

"Yes, say yes, and this will all be over." The purulent voice had an eager tone. "I will leave you in peace until I return to collect what is mine. This will all go away. I promise."

Wendell began to smell singed hair. "Y-y-y—"

The pain was unbearable, insufferable.

"Say it!"

His clothes began to smoke.

"Say it! Say it! Just say yes!"

"Y-y-you will never have my children!"

The thing cried out in a thunderous volume, a hurricane of saturated incantations from a nameless dialect.

The bronze bull rocked violently, which sent Wendell onto his back. In an instant the cloth was burned away, and his skin melted onto the white hot metal. He tried to scream, yet the air inside was now like a cauterizing iron. He felt like he had swallowed liquid steel that settled and hardened in his lungs, making breathing impossible. The smoke and fire from his burning clothes and flesh rose up in wispy columns on either side of him, as he screamed a silent scream.

6

Wendell was again pulled from the nightmare by a tug at his shoulder. He awoke with a start, flailing his arms about wildly.

"Whoa, whoa there, mister." The man backed away with his arms out ahead of him defensively. "Didn't mean to scare ya." He was a short, thin, middle-aged man with wild, dark hair all pushed to one side. A gray carpet of stubble covered a weathered face.

"Wha—. Where am I?" Wendell asked as he looked around him in fear and confusion.

"From the look of it," the man continued, "you're in the exact spot ya took your last step before ya done passed out, so ya are."

It was early morning, and there was a damp, chilly dew on the grass. A gray fog had settled in over the city from the lake, making anything over twenty feet away a gauzy specter in the wan light.

Feeling his limbs and back for scorched flesh and singed clothing, seeing there were none, Wendell breathed a sigh of relief. He gingerly pulled himself off the ground. "What time is it?" he asked the stranger.

"Jist past 7:30. Me and the missus live in the loft above my store there," he pointed to the brick two-story building to his right. "I was just coming down to empty me pot when I seen ya laying there. Well, boy, you musta tickled the bottom of the bottle with yer tongue last night, so ya must."

Slowly, his surroundings became familiar. He was in the weeded lot between the two buildings where he had stumbled and lost his light. There, to his right was the footpath. He could even see the root he'd tripped over with the votives laying on their sides nearby.

"Been years since I couldn't see the holes in a ladder, so it has. The missus, she don't take too kindly to drunkards. It was either her or the booze, she told me, so she did. Well, look at me. I ain't but a runt of a man, and not very afternoonified." He threw his hands up in the air, as if in defeat. "What could I do? So the missus won out over the whiskey. But what man wouldn't pick hooters over hooch, I ask."

Wishing to extricate himself from his new, extremely talkative acquaintance, Wendell just nodded and said, "And I'm sure it was the best decision you've ever made."

The man was about to go into another dissertation of some sort or other, but Wendell cut him off, "Thank you, sir, for rousing me. You've done me a great favor, one I hope I may be able to repay at a later time. However, last night's merriment has made me late for another appointment." He shook the man's hand vigorously then ran away before the man could respond, first picking up his votives, then sprinting towards the Reed House a block away, still reaching wildly at his arms and back.

· · · · ·

When the knock came at 8:45, Wendell was prepared. The early morning fog was not readily giving up its foothold on the area, and dark spaces clung like frightened children to any space not near a light source. He had relit the votives from the church and the four candles and oil lamp in the room. It wasn't the Presque Isle light house light but it would do.

Wendell answered the door, eagerly shook the priest's hand and motioned for him to enter.

"So how was your night?" Father Casey asked in anticipation, as he took a seat at the writing desk near the window.

Wendell couldn't sit, so he paced from window to bed to window again. He felt movement would keep his mind working and his senses sharper. He also needed to work off a fretful energy he'd had since he was aroused from his torturous dream. "Not so good," he replied after making a quick circuit.

"You fell asleep?"

"No, I tripped on my way back to the hotel and the candles went out. The thing in the shadows grabbed me." He shuddered but didn't finish the thought. There was really no reason to go into the details of what happened next.

The priest sensed the same thing and didn't push for any more particulars. He only said, "You didn't —"

"I didn't," Wendell interjected.

"Well, good for you,"

"No, good for them."

"Well, yes, you are right," Father Casey agreed sheepishly.

"So please. Let's cut the niceties and get down to it. What can you tell me about this creature?"

The priest drew a hesitant breath and began. "First, you should know that I have been researching mightily this creature that has attached itself to your family. Ever since your father first came to me I've been pouring over volumes, some quite ancient, in Monsignor's study. I dare say that some tomes might be as old as he is."

Wendell looked unpretentiously at the priest in his attempt at levity.

"Uh hem, yes, well I have found very little information on this *daemon parasitus.*"

Wendell stopped mid-step. "This what?"

"Sorry. You must remember that Christianity is very old, nearly two thousand years, and the study of demons has gone even longer when you factor in Jewish literature. They are categorized in families or types much the same way scientists categorize animals, plants or insects."

"You're losing me on this."

"Ok, think of, say, beetles, and bees, and spiders and crickets and such; they are all insects but they belong to different families or kinds of insects. Demons are classified much the same way, based on the kind of demon they are. The religious back then had more time on their hands to undertake such endeavors, apparently. Anyway, this particular kind of demon is classified as a *daemon parasitus* or parasitic demon. They latch onto a person and feed off its soul, like a parasite does to its host — think of a flea or tick or maybe mosquito when it latches onto an arm or neck. Unfortunately, very little is known about this genus of demon, or at least very little has been written about them in the volumes I've thus researched. They are some of the oldest demons recorded, only one or two generations removed from the Original Fall. The ancients called them the Niphilim. Their existence is well known by the religious; however their habits, how and why they attach themselves to people, and how to combat them — well, little seems to have been written about that, unfortunately. I came across this information only a few days ago, so the revelation wasn't much consolation to your father."

By this time, Wendell had stopped his frenetic pacing and took a seat on the edge of the bed, feet crossed underneath him. "Ok, that's a start."

"From what I've read they attach themselves and feed off the souls, which is different from the more familiar *possession* where the demon actually takes control of the body."

"How do we stop them from feeding? How do we stop them from moving on to whoever they want next?"

"Ah," Father Casey said, wagging his finger, "that is the next part of the puzzle that needs to be solved. It seems they cannot take another soul unless they are given permission. Even Satan and his minions have Providential Laws that must be followed — that much is clear. That seems to be the main purpose of this façade of torture."

"Façade my ass," Wendell disagreed. "Sorry, no offense intended."

The priest smiled. "None taken. You have to remember that you are coming out of these acts unscathed, physically, anyway, so all the torture you endure is made up. It may feel real in the moment — that I do not doubt; but its purpose is only to get your consent, nothing more. Remember, it already has your soul. Now it needs to think ahead to where its next meal is coming from. The simulated torture is this thing's mechanism of securing that."

Father Casey realized the last comment's consequence when Wendell's features suddenly sagged from subdued hope to melancholia. He tried to undo it. "Just because this demon has your soul does not in any way mean it is going to *keep* your soul. My purpose in this endeavor has always been two-fold and it will remain that, I assure you."

Recovering himself, if only slightly, Wendell asked, "So what happens if I don't give in? Will it go away?"

Father Casey sighed. "I honestly don't know. Maybe there are stories that I haven't yet come across that give an account of those that broke the cycle. I'm sure they are there. Now it is my singular duty to find them." There was an uncomfortably long silence before the priest spoke again. "I'm afraid that you are now completely up to date."

"That is all you know?"

"Believe it or not, that's quite a bit more that what your father knew."

"Well that hardly helps at all." Wendell got up and began his pacing, once again.

The priest rubbed his forehead broodingly, "I understand your frustration, but you must understand that this may take some time. I have a limited library from which to work, although I believe I will find our answers in it, and I have a limited amount of time in which to search. I can honestly tell you that almost every free minute that I have at my disposal is used in this one endeavor."

"Is there a possibility that you can change *almost* every free minute to actually all of them?"

"Monsignor has over two dozen volumes on demonology alone. I have been at this since your father came to me months ago and have only gotten through sixteen volumes. It was all I could do to find this information. I had never even heard of this kind of demon before I started on this journey."

Father Casey let out a heavy sigh, as though a great weight had been placed upon his chest. "I will do everything in my power to save you and your children. You must believe that. However, I ask that you, to the best of your ability, practice patience. If we are lucky you may yet win this battle. A battle just starting for you but one, may I remind you, your father fought silently for a very long time. As bleak as all seems right now, yours is a privilege your father did not get the chance to have."

The blade of that statement cut Wendell to the quick. But it was a necessary wound for it pulled him back from a fast-forming self-pity. "I apologize. I will persevere for as long as it takes to find the answers we need. I don't have a choice."

"Good."

Wendell and the priest walked to the door together. As Father Casey opened the door, he said, "I am going back to the parish to pour over some more volumes. Monsignor is visiting with the bishop for the entire day, so I should be able to work unencumbered. If I can find anything else that might be of help, I will come straight here with the news, I promise."

Wendell smiled weakly. "Thank you."

"I will not let you or your family down. We will get through this. I promise."

The priest's words had a forced conviction and as Wendell closed the door, he wondered if the priest was trying to convince himself more than Wendell of the statement's veracity.

Within an hour the sun had burned off the foggy veil, and Wendell felt safe enough to leave his room.

The air was chilly, which was a welcome and soothing feeling, as he ambled aimlessly through the streets. Even though the waking nightmare of the preceding night was only a "façade", and he had no visible burns, something inside him felt different. It seemed that each horror built upon the previous one, erecting a lead-weighted edifice in his stomach housed full of dread and ghastly uncertainty and unimaginable fear, not for him so much, but for his children, who he hadn't seen since they were babies.

In a haze that equaled anything from a pipe, and without even realizing it, his feet had unconsciously taken him in a familiar direction.

7

A half-hour's walk east along the ridgeline of the bay, past the mouth of Mill Creek, Wendell finally came upon a strip of old clapboard houses that straddled a dirt street with no name. These dwellings had once housed the workers of a saw mill. The mill had been deserted for some time, and the original tenants had long ago abandoned the row-houses in search of employment elsewhere. In their place were those of a social persuasion a gossamer's width higher than a pauper—they were the working poor.

Verity's small flat was at the near end of the row, under the decrepit umbrella of an ancient willow partly cleaved in the middle of its great trunk from weight and time. Its gnarled, weeping branches, half naked with yellowing leaves, were more dead than alive. Those autumn-parched patches cast uneven shadows across the chipped and graying whitewash. The dried skeletons of Queen Ann's Lace and Goldenrod poked up from cracks in the walkway and along the entire base of the row of houses.

Wendell had anticipated that Verity and the twins were home. A wisp of blue that flickered past a soot-blackened side window assured him his intuition hadn't erred.

He wasn't going to just knock and assert himself. He had no right. His children wouldn't know him, and Verity would more likely than not forbid him from crossing the threshold, anyway. He had broken her heart nearly four years ago and just showing up on her doorstep, contrite, could not change the past.

He left the dirt road for a more clandestine approach through the high weeds and overgrown shrubbery.

He would watch them vicariously through the window.

As he stalked through the browning weeds, Wendell came to the conclusion that the animals here had less than even their cousins in the wild, for at least those beasts had shelter and plenty to eat and lived out their lives contented until preyed upon by something higher on the food chain. In this forgotten spot, however, nothing was guaranteed — even to animals unlucky enough to have been domesticated. Here and there dead carcasses, some more recently deceased than others, littered his path to Verity's window. Wendell picked his way through them, slapping at hungry flies and desperate fleas searching out new blood on which to feed.

It seemed an odd paradox to Wendell — those unwanted, poor souls that society had thrown away, who themselves take in a stray dog or cat for amity and companionship but ultimately having to pick between feeding themselves or their new friends. This browning patch of weeds was a testament to whose will had been done.

Having finally slinked his way across the animal necropolis, Wendell pressed himself up against the rotting wood along the outer wall, next to the window.

Several muffled voices could be heard beyond the dirty glass, but Wendell's view was too acute to make anything out. He crept closer and dared to press his eyes to the glass.

Inside, to his left beyond an archway, were three children — two girls and a boy — sitting around a small table, happily keeping themselves busy with childish gibberish and laughing playfully. A fourth younger girl with matted hair and a dirty face was sitting on the floor watching the other three.

He recognized immediately Abel and Becca at the table; they were the older of the children. They had their mother's dark, Mediterranean features but Wendell's blue eyes and curly hair. However beautiful they were in his eyes, he couldn't help but notice the shallow cheeks, the bony hands and legs, the gray hue to their skin — the general disposition of the malnourished.

His breath caught in his throat, and his eyes welled with tears. Their ill circumstance was his fault. He had abandoned them when they most needed him. Although he suffered emotionally for that idiotic choice — suffering that was only ever alleviated temporarily by opium — they suffered doubly, for they lacked both the love of a father and his ability to keep them fed.

Suddenly, from around a corner in the room, a young, dark-haired woman appeared with a plate and a small, round loaf of cut bread. She set it on the table and gave a slice to the girl on the floor, while the others each grabbed a dry slice and began to eat hungrily. It was Verity. She still had most of her youthful beauty, however she looked beaten and tired on that emaciated frame. It was obvious by the look of her that she was letting the children eat while she went without. His time away from them now sickened him at his heart.

The two other children looked nothing like Verity or the twins; they were pale and each had stringy blond hair. Wendell looked as best he could into the other rooms to see if another woman could be glimpsed at another task, but the rest of the flat looked empty. He decided that the mother of the younger children was probably at work somewhere. Husband-less women often pooled their resources, watching each other's children while the other worked. Some of the luckier ones would even convince their bosses to let them split a ten hour shift with a friend so one of them would be at home at all times to take care of the children. They each got paid less but the two together made the wages of one. It wasn't ideal, but it helped many families survive, if only barely.

Instead of coming here and surreptitiously ruminating on a once happier time of his life to make himself feel better, he now felt worse. An air of utter incompetence was beginning to overwhelm him.

He peered out over browning landscape to regather himself, as he wiped tears from his cheeks.

If all that wasn't enough, he doubted he had the stamina his father possessed to keep his children from the clutches of the demon in the darkness. He no longer cared about himself. He would gladly spend eternity in its clutches to spare his boy and girl. Yet, he couldn't begin to fathom the year of torture his own father had endured for him of the magnitude that Wendell had endured in just this one night passed. The priest might be able to find an answer in those ancient books. He seemed confident he would. Wendell had his doubts. If Father Casey did, however, somehow figure this out, he feared the revelation would come too late.

A heavy, stuttered sigh later he put his eyes back to the window. He would afford one last glimpse before heading back into town and waiting with utter impatience for word on any headway made by the priest. It was then that he saw it: In the corner of the room behind the children at the table, in the caliginous murk between two bare cupboards on the joining walls, the shadows moved. It was like a slick mass of rain-soaked earth with worms fighting to its surface.

Wendell's heart skipped a beat.

Verity walked to the table, took up the plate of bread from the children, and placed it in one of those empty cupboards, seemingly unaware of the thing in the shadows. It appeared she was looking right at the demon without so much as a gasp or startle. Then he remembered that his father had tried to show Father Casey, but he had been unable to see it. Wendell concluded that the monstrosity must only show itself to those it is tormenting, or — part of the Providential Law the priest had spoken of — it can only be seen by them.

As soon as Verity moved away from the cupboard to attend another task out of his view, he could see the thing more clearly. Its vomitous eyes were now open, and it cast its unholy gaze down at the children. The putrid glow of them brightened, as if in anticipation. Then those disgusting sockets shot at once to Wendell at the window. A thin jagged line, like black lightning, appeared in the oily space under those eyes; it had bared a contemptuous, stygian grin at him, which quick-froze his marrow.

It knew he was there. Maybe, Wendell thought, it was only there because he was. It manifest itself in the presence of his children only to torment him. In a way, its nearness to them now anguished him more than being burned alive in some demented torture chamber.

Suddenly, something unexpected happened. His fear was quickly replaced with anger — a protective anger that any man should have when harm presented itself to his children. A righteous anger for what is true and good when evil and corruption prevailed.

Then, unaccountably, something else presented itself; something for which he was not prepared — a thought. The seeds of an idea that seemed to be watered by his wrath began to sprout in the fertile field of his mind. A concatenation of things said and things seen. In that moment, for reasons unknown to him, Wendell thought he had found a way to defeat the demon.

No longer caring for surreptitiousness, He ran from the window, through the high weeds, and back onto the dirt road. Once out of sight from the dilapidated row houses, he lessened his sprint to a fast walk and headed back towards town, all the while with a gritty determination affixed to his face. There were things needing put into place before his plan came to fruition.

Come nightfall, he would rid his family of this demon for good. That reflection at last made him smile.

8

Father Casey unfastened his reading glasses and pushed the open volume away in frustration. He pinched at his nose and tried to blink clearness back into his eyes. Four other volumes were splayed open, cluttered across his desk.

Nothing. He'd found nothing. He was beginning to think that maybe these books did not contain the answers he needed, though several more books lay unopen at his feet. He'd heard that Saint Vincent Seminary in Latrobe had quite an extensive library for its seminarians. That would be his next recourse if these proved fruitless.

He pulled out his pocket watch and clicked it open: 6:10 pm. He wasn't surprised monsignor had yet to return from visiting the bishop, because, quite frankly, it might be one of the last times the two old friends would meet in this life. Lately, the old man's gate had gotten more unsteady and painful, and Father Casey figured it wouldn't be long before he would take to his bed for good.

The priest decided he would go spend the night with Wendell. He would keep vigil with him during this second troubling night, since he was no help to the man on his first.

As he left his study, he passed by a nun reading on a settee in front of a small fire in the common room of the rectory. She was monsignor's nurse. Although she was reading, she had a worried look on her face.

Appraising the look Father Casey said, "Don't worry, sister. Monsignor will be home soon."

Looking up she said, "He should have let me go with him. I wouldn't have been a bother. What if he needs me?"

"Oh, you know him. He just wanted to have one last night with the bishop as a friend and not as a co-laborer. They are probably sitting in the parlor smoking cigars and rehashing old war stories. They were both at Gettysburg, you know — one as a soldier and one as a chaplain."

"Now that's something to talk about," she said admonishingly.

The priest pulled on the overcoat he grabbed from a coatrack next to the door. "When he returns will you tell him that I am visiting a friend whose father just died. I may not be back till morning."

"But . . . but I'll be here with him alone. That is not proper."

"Sister, Jesus let a woman kiss his feet because he knew her intentions were holy. I really don't think the good Lord will hold it against you being alone in monsignor's company for, what—a half hour, forty minutes, to get him ready for bed before you retire to your room."

Shaking her head vigorously, the nun said, "I really don't think it right and proper to leave me here unattended."

He smiled in that gentle and warming way he was known for. "Sometimes the rules have to be bent, even if just a little, when exorcising the duties to which we are called. This soul cannot wait. He needs comforting. Do I neglect him out of social decorum?"

She thought it over for a moment. "No, I suppose not. But it still makes me very uncomfortable."

"May I suggest you offer it up in prayer." With that, Father Casey left the rectory and stepped out into a growing twilight.

. . . .

Wendell sat in a nervous anticipation in front of the curtained window of his room. The place was already in a dark gray pall, and in only a few more moments darkness would fully consume it.

Next to him on the writing desk was a candle. Wendell had previously trimmed the wick until it was just above the wax. He lit it, and the diminutive flame barely cut through the gloom—just as he wanted.

He pulled from within his suitcoat the pocket watch which he had taken from his father's room the day before. It shook gently in his hand, yet he was not afraid. Events, however severe, never dictated a body's need for more opium. This time it would not get what it so desperately wanted. He traced the smooth gold of the watch as best he could with his fingertips. He didn't open it for the time; the time did not matter. He held it for strength. A strength he did not possess in and of himself but needed now more than ever.

He waited for the demon.

A few minutes later, the darkness awakened.

A moment after, the yellow eyes found life in that turbid froth.

"Good evening, Mr. Wiggins," it said in a speech that sounded like broken glass being trampled underfoot. "Are you prepared for this evening? I have been waiting anxiously for us to play some more."

"I am ready," Wendell replied with steely determination. "But let us have a conversation first. We have time. As you said, eternity is pregnant with it. So let's chat first."

It was silent for a long moment, as if ascertaining an underlying motive for the request. "As you wish," it finally said.

It crept closer to Wendell but still stayed in the darker shadows, at first.

Wendell placed the watch on his lap and crossed his arms. "Why have you attached yourself to my family?" he asked, trying to conceal a quiver in his speech.

"Why not?" it replied. "You are no better or worse than anyone else. The decision was made many centuries ago with no consideration to the *who* or the *why*. It just is."

"What did you do to my father's soul when he died?"

"It might be easier to show you than to tell you."

The thing then approached the lesser gloom, giving Wendell the first opportunity to glimpse in fuller detail its grotesqueness. It had an ill-defined form that approached that of a large, misshapen man. The surface of the thing was blacker than the shadows it occupied and had an unctuous shell that oozed like liquid mercury. However, the most horrific part of the thing was the large, bulging protuberances that appeared and melted back into its body, like a bubble forming on hot tar that doesn't break but is absorbed back into the molten liquid.

At first, Wendell pressed back into his chair in fear that one of these pustules would pop and splash some ghoulish acid onto his face that would eat its way into his brain. But what he saw on a more deliberate inspection made his first thought seem pedestrian. Faces could be seen within those bosselations, pressing against the membranous skin of the thing with wild exasperations of horror on their faces. It was as though they were trying yet failing to escape it. One of those faces was that of his father. To his horror, another was that of his mother.

Wendell gasped, and his mind spun uncontrollably. It was his mother who had passed the demon to his father. The thought sickened him.

That revelation and Wendell's reaction made the creature snort out a gleeful resonance like that of a train crash. "You really must be careful what you wish for."

With every ounce of fortitude that coursed through his body, Wendell regained himself. There was still something which needed done, and that disclosure would not hinder his plan. He said, "Well, your reign over this family has come to an end."

. . . .

Father Casey stopped outside Wendell's hotel room door. He was about to knock but heard Wendell in conversation with someone. At first, he thought that Wendell had already found a friend with whom to pass the night. However, when he heard no replies from the guest, he felt something wasn't right.

He stood silently and listened.

An audible gasp came from within.

He tried the doorknob but it was locked

The priest began to pound on the door. "Wendell. Wendell, it is Father Casey. Wendell!"

There was no reply.

. . . .

Wendell only looked in the direction of the door but made no attempt to answer it.

The thing inched closer to Wendell. It was now at the feeble edge of candle light. An impossibly black, taloned hand whose fingers tapered to razor sharp points reached, not through the border of candlelight, but around its perimeter. The appendage just stretched longer, impossibly longer along that murky edge between the light and dark.

It was then that Wendell realized that his entire right side was in the shadow created by his own body from the candlelight to his left.

"Do you think you are the first to try and break my bond?" the demon remonstrated. "You are not. The souls I have is a testament to that. I am eternal. My reign cannot end."

. . . .

Father Casey began to kick violently at the door. "Wendell! Wendell, don't say yes! Don't give in!" It took four kicks before the wooden frame began to splinter. Two more kicks, and the wooden door relented.

The priest rushed into the room.

. . . .

"You may be eternal," Wendell replied. "But I am not."

From within his suitcoat Wendell produced a revolver.

At first, the creature's eyes brightened as if amused that the man would try to snuff it out in such a fatuous way. But when Wendell put the gun to his temple the demon's features changed altogether.

Wendell heard two voices scream "No!" Then he pulled the trigger.

. . . .

The gunshot sent Father Casey to his knees. In such a confined space the peal stung his ears. A moment later, all was quiet except a ringing that would not go away. In the flicker of anemic candlelight the aftermath could be seen on the walls over the writing desk.

Looking around, as he picked himself off the floor, there was no one and nothing else in the room. Only himself and Wendell.

He rushed to the body and said a hasty prayer in Latin.

Afterwards, he whispered, "I am truly sorry I wasn't more help to you — you and your family."

As he was making a sign of the cross over Wendell, he glimpsed a blood-spiculed envelope on the other side of the candle. On it was scribbled *Father Casey.*

Epilogue

As he readied himself for bed, Father Casey solemnly recollected the events of the last week. He stared at himself in the flickered cast-off light from the candle through the mirror. He looked no different but felt as though he had aged two decades. He had put a father and a son in the ground, which was tragic enough. However, the reasons behind their deaths, and his inability to help them when they came to him, made the events an even more unpleasant pill to swallow.

He looked beside him at the letter Wendell had left behind. Its contents were really the only thing of any consequence that made his failure at least tolerable. In it, he had revealed that he'd visited his father's lawyer and signed over his entire inheritance, $55,000, to Verity and his two children. Wendell wanted him to be the one to give them the good news.

It had turned out to be sad news, as well. If only Wendell had known that Verity cried. That she had never stopped loving him and always held out hope that he'd return one day. She never knew the extent of his addiction to opium, which was the official cause of his suicide.

The priest let out a melancholy sigh, which was used to snuff the candle. So much of the truth would never be known. No one would know Wendell's death before relenting to the demon would in turn save his children from his fate and the fate of his father and mother and untold people before that.

Tired, he got up from his desk and walked in the darkness to his bed.

It was then that he heard a strange voice coming from everywhere but nowhere. "Oh, Father Casey. What pains I have in store for you!"

Bumps in the Night

When Papa brought the stranger home that January evening, I knew something bad was going to happen. It always did. Not at first. First, there would be eating and story-telling, as Papa and the man would get to know each other better. The man, usually homeless by the way he dressed and smelled, would tell Papa about what he'd done before he became homeless. Papa would listen intently as the man would describe how hard and joyless life had become. Papa was genuinely interested in every man's story. He felt sorry for them and how they got that way. That is why he did to them what he did — to stop their suffering. He told me so and I believe him.

Before I give you this current story I must back track and give you a bit of my past story. Papa is a wealthy man. His father before him made a fortune in the oil fields of western Pennsylvania after the first successful oil wells were dug. Papa inherited that fortune. I never knew Mama. She died giving birth to me. Papa tells me she was a wonderful woman. Whenever he speaks of her I see tears in his eyes. He always tell me that it's just smoke from the fireplace irritating his eyes, even when we are in a room with no fireplace. I may be dumb, but I am not stupid; he misses her every day.

I say that I may be dumb, but I am not stupid because I was born with Down Syndrome. The doctors told Papa to get rid of me, but he saw Mama in my eyes and has kept me and loved me no matter what. He has me taught as best as I could be taught. He never looks at me funny, like most people do, and he plays with me every day. He is my best and only friend, besides my two baby dolls and two wooden spoons I pretend are baby dolls.

You might be wondering how Papa, who seems to be a very loving person, could do what he does to the homeless people he brings home. As I said, he wants to end their suffering. Plus he needs them—for food.

See, one day a long time ago when I was just a little girl, he went hunting with friends. Something terrible happened. He was attacked by an animal, though he never told me what kind. I am sure it was big and hairy with lots of teeth and yellow eyes and sharp claws — at least that is how I pictured it as he told the story. He was scratched and bitten all over his body, but he healed well and recovered quickly. But from that point on, once a month when the moon was big and fat in the sky, something bad would happen to Papa. I never got to see it but boy did I hear it.

Eventually, I overheard Papa and some friends talking about people in the community being caught after dark and eaten by some unseen monster. Papa feared for me, and since I myself have an aversion to monsters of any stripe, we decided to move far away. It wasn't until finding out that monster had followed us to our new town that I figured out all by myself that it might have had something to do with Papa and his attack.

He eventually confided in me about his monthly *transformations* when the moon outside was full. It wasn't his fault. He didn't want to do it but couldn't stop himself, either.

He had said more than once that he had thought about going to the place where Mama is. He said he had more than enough silver to do it. I took that to mean that silver could kill you, so after he told me that I switched out our good silverware for stainless steel. As much as I miss

Mama, I am not ready to go where she is. I hear it's a long trip. Anyway, Papa said he couldn't do that because he couldn't leave me alone, which I am grateful for. He said I would end up in a large building with soft walls and no pictures, where everyone wears white clothes all the time, and no one will like me, and they would treat me bad. Sometimes when I think about it, I feel bad for the people who are in these terrible places and I cry, for no one loves them the way Papa loves me.

So it is for that reason that he stays here to take care of me, with the once-a-month dinner guest the only part I don't like.

That brings me back to our latest guest. He and Papa got along splendidly. His name was Hugh, and he was a veteran of the Great War. Papa and Hugh traded stories all through dinner with lots of laughing and old recollections. The beggar was polite and seemed very smart for being in his particular circumstance, but he also smelled like sardines. His clothing hung loosely about him, but he didn't seem as skinny and feeble as most of the other dinner guests. He seemed to be embarrassed about his situation and apologized often of that fact. His life seemed more thrust upon him than a choice he made due to drink or drugs or mental defect like mine.

After dinner Papa hugged me, kissed me gently on my chubby cheek, then asked the man, Hugh, to go with him into the study to smoke a cigar. I knew then that it was time for me to go to my room. I will never forget the look he gave me that night when he kissed me goodnight; it was a mixture of sadness and regret and hopelessness. Underlying them was that malevolent sparkle that animals have when the light hits them just right. They had begun to change color from the bright blue to that of a greenish hue that I cannot accurately describe.

The transformation was about to begin.

It was only a little past 7:00, but the night had fallen some time ago. I looked out the window on the landing on the way to my room, and already I could see the full moon. It was still close to the ground so it looked even bigger than when it's higher in the sky.

Soon the transformation would completely take over, and Papa would get hungry again. I felt bad for the homeless man, more so than the others, though I felt bad for all of them. He got along so well with Papa. He didn't have many friends besides me, and I always felt bad that he had to talk to me. I do my best but regular people need to have regular conversations with other regular people, not with those who talk to wooden spoons.

I got ready for bed then closed the thick, heavy door and secured the four separate deadbolt locks. I grabbed my two baby dolls and the two wooden spoons I pretend are baby dolls, struggled under the thick blankets of my bed and waited nervously for the bumps in the night.

There are always bumps in the night of a full moon. Shortly after that, the screaming starts, but it doesn't last long. I don't know why the screaming doesn't start before the bumps, but I was told that curiosity killed the cat and though I am not a cat, I love them and don't want to be killed by proxy.

I must have dozed off because the bumps startled me back awake. If my dolls had been dandelions, their heads would have popped off and fell to the floor. It was after 9:00, and just outside my window the yellowish glow of the moon was making its way past my window sill.

I listened intently, dolls and spoons ready to give me comfort for what was to follow. There was another bump of such force I could feel my bed shudder slightly underneath me. There was almost never more than two bumps before the screaming started so I sunk my head deeper into my pillow to muffle the cries. It is those cries and screams and gurgling sounds that scare me the most. The howls and growls that I know are Papa—not so much anymore.

What happened next changed my life forever. I was expecting the shrieks and cries to echo through the big house, but what I heard was the muffled *crack*, like a firecracker going off. I heard three more before all went quiet.

As I lay in bed playing with my baby dolls and the spoons I pretend are baby dolls in the silence that usually accompanied Papa's second dinner, I suddenly heard a knock at my door.

"Alina?" the voice asked shakily.

When I realized that it was not Papa, for he wouldn't go back to his old self till morning, I called through the thick door, "You are supposed to be dead and eaten. Why are you outside my room?"

"Child, I think there is something you need to know," the homeless man said rather sadly.

"I know enough to know that I am not supposed to open this door again until morning," I replied in no uncertain terms.

"If you are afraid of your father you needn't worry anymore. He's…he's dead."

At that moment, my heart sank so deep into my chest that it pulled my lungs with it making it difficult to breathe. The only person who ever loved me, despite my affliction and his own, was now gone. Gone to where Momma was, and I was there all alone.

My dolls and spoons fell to the floor with a dull *thud*.

"Please open the door," the man pleaded in a gentle tone I had only heard from Papa. "There's something I need to show you."

I paused a moment to let the finality of it sink in and tears welled I my eyes. I almost couldn't unlatch the deadbolts, but slowly, one by one, I unlocked the door.

The homeless war veteran was standing in front of me. He still had both arms, both legs, and no internal organs showed through his stinky clothes. To my surprise there were tears in his eyes, too. In his hand he held a letter. "Your dad left this for you. Can you read?"

"I may be dumb but I'm not stupid," I replied through my tears.

"Of course. I apologize."

He handed me the letter. It trembled in my hand as I struggled mightily to read what it said; but I was determined to have this moment between me and Papa without help.

My dearest daughter,

Once you receive this letter I will be dead. I am sorry that I hid this from you but couldn't bear the thought of seeing how it would affect you. I can no longer take the strain of my wolfen affliction and can't stomach another killing. I have been torn for years between my duty to you as a father and ending my life to save the innocent people I kill as a werewolf. Because I refuse to put you in an institution I have been committed these last few months to finding someone suitable for a dual purpose – that of killing me and looking after you. It was a very hard task, but I believe I have found that person in Hugh Stover. He has the steely war-hardened nerves to fulfill the first and the kindness and compassion to fulfill the second. It was that combination that I sought out and would not put my plan into place until I had. Rest assured, my little one, that I am no longer in torment. Mama and

I can watch you grow up happy without having to lock your bedroom door anymore. Please do not hate Mr. Stover. He only did what I had asked him to do. I hope you will grow to love him like a father. Just remember, what he did – what I had asked him to do – was for the best, even if you can't see it right now. Loving you and missing you with all my heart.

Papa

I looked at the strange man with swollen eyes, not knowing what to do or say.

"I made a promise to take care of you," the man, Hugh, said. "I promise to do my best for you."

"Do you even know how to take care of someone – someone like me?"

He squatted down to my level because he was a very tall man. "Well, once I had a wife and a little girl just a bit younger than you are now."

"Where are they? Will they be coming to stay here too?"

The man's face distorted into an even sadder expression than the one he currently wore and said, "They died in a car accident while I was away at war."

"So I guess we both have a reason to be sad." I wiped the tears from my cheek. "So what happens now?"

"Your dad took care of all the details. We can stay here or we can move to another house. I'll let you decide, but for now you need to try and go back to bed and get some rest while I—take care of things down stairs."

I nodded solemnly. I would miss Papa dearly, but I knew how much his affliction bothered him. The last thing I wanted was for him and Mama to be unhappy on account of me. This man, Hugh, seemed to share some of the loss I felt. I know Papa would do everything in his power to make sure the person who took care of me was a kind and loving person. I trusted Papa in death as I had done in life.

He rested his big hands on my shoulders and looked me square in the eye the way only one other person ever had. "As hard as it might be to get some rest, please try and leave everything else to me, okay?"

I nodded and wiped my runny nose.

As he rose, Hugh squinted in pain and grabbed his side. It was then that I saw the blood stain. It must have taken a while to seep through all his layers of clothes.

"Are you alright?" I asked.

He only smiled. "Your father was faster than I had expected. I guess he got a nip in before I had a chance to…" He didn't finish the sentence, just winked and smiled and said, "I'm fine. Now you go and get some rest while I attend to things down stairs."

When he turned and gingerly walked back down the hallway holding his side, when he disappeared down the stairs to do whatever tasks he and Papa had planned, I thought to myself that he and Papa were now more alike than anyone could ever have imagined.

It has been a year since that terrible night when my heart died. Me and Hugh moved to another home near the cemetery where Papa is buried so I can visit and tell him I how much I love him and miss him. I still have my two baby dolls and my two wooden spoons I pretend are baby dolls—and I still have the locks on my door to keep out the bumps in the night.

It's Just Johnny

The cry from the other room woke up the woman. She wiped a tangle of hair from her eyes with one hand while she nudged her husband with the other, who barely registered the interruption. "Did you hear that?" she asked. "Timothy? Did you hear that noise?"

Smacking his lips sleepily, the man mumbled, "It's just Johnny. He'll go back to sleep." He rolled over taking most of the covers with him.

She pulled them back in irritation and began to readjust herself in the well-worn bed when there was another, louder cry.

Nudging the man's shoulder once more she said, "I think he's having a nightmare."

The second cry roused the man more fully from his slumber. Rubbing her pumpkin-sized abdomen from under the covers he said, "You two stay here. I'll go check on him."

"You're a dear," she replied and kissed his shoulder.

She readjusted herself under the warm covers, as he slowly maneuvered himself from the mattress.

He lit a candle on his nightstand and staggered in a sleepy crawl down the hallway to the six year old's room.

The door protested noisily when the father entered Johnny's room. The little boy was sitting up in his bed with the threadbare covers pulled up over his head. There was a visible shake in the old, stained bedding.

The father noticed the window on the opposite wall was open, letting in filaments of cold October night. "Johnny, why on earth do you have the window open? You'll catch your death in that chill."

Without waiting for a reply, he went to the window and looked out into the night. Fingers of fog strangled the closer trees and clung in hazy clumps to the lower dales and wood line farther out, next to the graveyard. The full moon glowed phosphorescently in the high starlit sky. The whole nightscape was one of an eerie, gothic composition that gave him goosebumps.

He shuddered briefly then shut the window and turned back to his son. "So why did you cry out? Did you have a nightmare?"

A skinny, sheet-covered arm only pointed under the bed, as he gave a frightened whimper.

"Oh, so there's a monster under your bed?" the father asked trying to hide a smile.

The covers vigorously shook in the affirmative.

With a sleepy grin the dad asked, "So if I look under the bed and make sure there are no monsters under there, you'll go back to sleep?"

The covers nodded yes.

The dad went to the bed, got on his hands and knees, placed the candle on the floor and bent down to look underneath.

The shock of what he saw didn't immediately register; he just knelt there in wide-eyed confusion at first, then suddenly in stark terror. His son was shaking uncontrollably in the darkly shadowed space. When the boy's teary eyes met his father's he whispered with dreadful fear, "Daddy, there's something in my bed."

Suddenly, the man felt something cold and wet clamping around his neck, cutting off a scream.

Made in the USA
Lexington, KY
26 November 2017